Conjuring Cupcakes: A Paranormal Culinary Cozy Mystery

The Misadventures of a Cat Detective Series

Contents

1

THE TEA PARTY

The Parkson's mansion in Hivensrock loomed over us as we drove through the iron gates. I felt a shiver run down my spine as I remembered the last time I was here. It was six months ago when Diana had been hired to bake for the opening of Colleen Parkson's theater. Right before our eyes - and the eyes of a hundred other Hivensrock citizens - the man had been killed and his murderer turned out to be his illegitimate son.

Now, Helena, his wife, had hired Diana and me again to let our bakery, Charlotte's Treats, throw a tea party for her birthday. She said it was a way of thanking us for solving her husband's murder. I wasn't here for another mystery, but I knew what lay beneath the Parkson's mansion. It was the Dark Stone, a powerful artifact that had been the cause of several deaths and problems in both Picklesquare and Hivensrock.

Diana and I got out of the car, carrying the cakes and pastries we had made – Helena was providing the tea cups and kettles (and the tea, too). We wore our aprons and our smiles, ready to make Helena Parkson happy. I never knew all those months ago when I inherited (Insert name of the manor she inherited here) in Picklesquare that I'd be embroiled in an ancient mystery that involved not only my ancestors but many of the town's historic unsolved murder cases. I wondered if we could convince Helena to hand over the Dark Stone and end its existence once and for all. Knowing that the stone could bring an evil spirit into this world but was hidden away by her recently deceased husband, I wasn't ready to delve into a maze underneath her home in hopes of finding the Dark Stone and destroying it.

Especially not with those huge alligators guarding it. The thought made me shiver.

We walked up the steps and rang the doorbell. The door opened and Helena greeted us with a hug. She wore a red silk dress that draped over her curves and a pearl necklace that matched her earrings. She looked elegant and sophisticated, as she always did.

"Charlotte, Diana, I'm so glad you're here," she gushed warmly, a bit out of character for her. "You look sharp."

"Thank you, Helena. You look beautiful," I said with a genuine smile, glad to see her in better spirits than the last time we spoke. "Happy birthday!"

"Thank you, dear. Come in, come in. The guests are already here. Let me introduce you to them."

I was surprised by Helena's warm welcome. The last time we had met, she had been cold and distant, almost disgusted by our presence. We'd also had a tough time interrogating her son, Matthew Parkson, and I was beyond glad that he was now out of the country, and therefore not in the way of whatever progress we might make with the Dark Stone.

Helena guided us into the living room where a cozy fire crackled in the fireplace. The walls were adorned with gilded paintings and portraits of different people, all of whom I guessed were past or present Parksons. The furniture was elegant and comfortable, with cushions and throws in rich colors. A dozen people lounged on the sofas and chairs, sipping wine and nibbling on cheese. They all turned their heads to the doorway as we entered, their expressions revealing their curiosity.

Helena smiled and waved at them. "Everyone, meet Charlotte and Diana, the planners for my tea party birthday celebration today. Charlotte and her friend, Detective Grey, solved Cole's murder and caught his killer. They are amazing, aren't they?"

The guests began to mutter, whispering to each other with a few of them even clapping, wide smiles on their faces. Some of them leaned forward as if to take us in better, eyes roving over us with unrestrained curiosity. Others showed no reaction at all, sitting demurely in their chairs and taking measured sips of wine or bites of cheese while eyeing

us. Helena for her part smiled widely, looking proud of us, for whatever reason.

The whole thing made me feel like a rare specimen in a zoo, and
I could feel Diana shifting beside me. I did my best not to show my
discomfort and lifted the tray of pastries for all to see.

"We've brought the tea things and an abundance of pastries – mac-
aroons, scones, sponge cakes, little cupcakes, if anyone wants a bite,"
I announced.

Diana chimed in, "And soon, we'll have tea, too."

"I do hope we won't be having tea made from tea bags?" a woman
sitting at the far end of the room said, shuddering as she said the words
"tea bags." I wanted to roll my eyes at how snooty she was being, but
before I could allay her fears, Helena stepped forward with a polite
smile that didn't reach her eyes.

"Megan, of course not! Have I ever served you anything you didn't
like?"

I looked between them, as did the other guests, some of them
snickering under their breath. It was safe for me to assume that not
only was there some tension here, it wasn't anything new, either.

The now-named Megan reddened and waved her hand furiously,
dismissing the sentiment laced within Helena's words.

"Of course not, dear Helena. I didn't mean to insinuate anything,
of course. I was just saying that the caterers might not—"

"They're *planners*, Megan." She looked like she had more to say, but she pursed her lips instead and turned back to us. The last look I got of Megan before I focused on Helena was her sinking back into her chair and the woman sitting next to her patting her hand.

"Anyway, ladies, I'll show you into the kitchen and then you can get started. This way, please."

She led us around the chairs and into the large kitchen, turning to us when we walked into the kitchen after her.

"I've already gotten the filtered water." She gestured to a large dispenser sitting at the end of the kitchen counter and pointed to the boxes on the table. "And the tea leaves. Diana, you can set up the pastries on the tea stand over there, and... I think that's it. You can bring the tea and pastries out whenever you're ready to serve. Any questions?"

I looked at Diana, but she was already shaking her head.

"Thank you, Helena. We'll take it from here."

Helena smiled brightly at that and nodded. "That's what I like to hear. If you have any questions at all, though, don't hesitate to come find me."

We nodded and she left the kitchen almost immediately. Diana and I looked at each other.

"Well," Diana said, smiling awkwardly. "That wasn't weird at all."

I laughed. "I know, right? Let's just do our thing so we can be out of here as soon as possible."

She agreed, and we got to work. Diana placed her pastries on the center table, and I did the same, taking them out of the tray and carefully arranging them in the tea stand.

Diana began boiling the water, filling three large kettles from the dispenser and then heating them on the burners. Initially we'd debated heating the water in the microwave because it would take less time, but even bringing the idea up had horrified Helena. So we were boiling the water instead, so it would be more "authentic."

I had just placed the last scone at the very top of the tea stand when one of the guests stepped into the room. A dark-haired woman in a chiffon flower-patterned dress smiled brightly at us as we stared at her.

"Uh, hi? Can we help you?" Diana said, putting the kettle she was about to lift off the burner back down. The woman shook her head and stepped further into the room.

"No, not really. I just got sick of the whole atmosphere in there." She waved vaguely behind her. "And I needed to go somewhere quiet for a bit. You don't mind, do you?"

I shook my head, and Diana gave her a small but kind smile. "We don't mind," she said. "We're nearly done here anyway."

The woman brightened up even more. I didn't think it was possible but it was in fact possible for someone to be that lively. The woman joined me at the table. She pulled one of the stools around the table to her side and plopped onto it, watching us with obvious interest.

"Oh, where are my manners!" she said about a minute after sitting at the table and just watching us. "I haven't introduced myself. You're Charlotte and Diana, right?"

I nodded at her, and Diana gave her another smile.

"We are," Diana said. "You got our names right, too."

The woman grinned at us. "I know you two, actually."

That got my interest. "You do?"

She nodded. "You guys are the ones behind Charlotte's Treats, aren't you? I've popped in a few times—your stuff is really good."

"Thank you," Diana and I said simultaneously, looking at each other with wide eyes and dissolving into giggles. I was feeling a lot more charitable towards the strange woman who had burst into the kitchen and so I asked for her name.

"So what's your name? I can't remember seeing you around, sorry, and it seems like you're new to Picklesquare?" I looked at Diana, who shook her head, confirming that she'd never seen her either.

"You're right. I've been in Picklesquare for... two weeks?" She scrunched up her button nose, her gaze trailing to the ceiling like she was trying to remember something. Then she nodded, seemingly sure of the answer.

"Yeah, two weeks. I'll be staying with Helena for a while. Oh, silly me—I still haven't introduced myself, have I?" She sat up and held her hand out for me to shake.

"Hi, I'm Rachel—Rachel Burke. I'm Helena's cousin—a distant one, though. She never stops reminding me about that. I'm also an animal whisperer."

I forced my expression to remain pleasant, even though I desperately wanted to lift my eyebrows and give her a skeptical look. After everything we'd gone through, nothing really surprised me anymore, but it seems there would always be an exception.

Diana, to her credit, didn't give Rachel any strange looks. Instead she said, "An animal whisperer? That sounds like it would be pretty cool. How does it work?"

Rachel opened her mouth, but before she could give us her answer Helena came into the room and inspected us, looking less than pleased.

"Rachel, you're not supposed to be in here with my planners, distracting them. Charlotte, Diana, the guests are starting to wonder if the tea will ever be ready."

I fought the urge to roll my eyes. I knew the grumpy Helena we'd met when her husband died was somewhere under the pleasant façade she'd put on, and I wasn't surprised it was coming out at last. I turned to her with my best customer service smile.

"Sorry about that, Helena. We're nearly done. All that's left is the tea, and the water's almost boiling. The leaves need to steep for a few minutes and then we can finally bring the tea out—"

"Yes, yes, I know how the process of making tea works. Just don't take more time than you have to, that's all."

She pivoted on her two-inch heels and left the room, leaving us looking at each other, bemused. Rachel got to her feet with a grunt.

"Well, that's my cue to leave, I guess. Sorry for putting you guys in trouble with your client," she said, scratching at her arm. As she did so she pushed the sleeve of the dress up, exposing a small red tattoo on her wrist for a brief moment. It was a strange drawing of two arcs intersecting in the middle, like someone had taken a Venn diagram of two interlocking circles and cut out the bottom half, leaving only the top half. The arcs were surrounded by lines going out from them like sun rays, and a horizontal line under the whole thing capped everything off. It was strange, but I thought it fit Rachel somehow.

"No worries," Diana said, smiling at her. "We know how Helena is, and it's not as bad as it looks."

"Are you sure?" Rachel asked, sounding worried for our wellbeing.

I smiled at her. "Positive."

She nodded and left us to our work.

2

DEADLY TEA

After we'd arranged everything according to how Helena wanted it and she was finally satisfied with how it looked, we finally set everything on two large trolleys and wheeled them out into the living room. The guests sat up eagerly, some looking more interested than others, but all of them followed our progress with their eyes as we moved into the center of the room.

The table had already been cleared out by Helena's housekeeper, whom I hadn't been able to speak to yet, and we quickly set up, placing the tea stand in the center of the table and putting the teapots and tea cups on the table where everyone could reach them. Then we stepped back after making sure everything was where it was supposed to be. We let Helena do the honors as she walked to the center of the room, standing just next to the table and clapping her hands together.

"Ladies, gentlemen." She nodded to the few men in the room who chuckled in the background. "The tea is finally here, and so, let the tea party officially begin!"

There was no loud cheering, but instead they clapped once or twice and then everyone got up from their seats and made their way to the table, getting their cups and pouring the tea themselves. It was more of a tea buffet than a tea party, to be honest, but there were so many guests that a regular tea party might not have worked. Diana and I waited by the table, making sure everyone got whatever type of tea they wanted and anyone who had any issues could get help, but eventually Helena asked us to take our own cups of tea and sit down when all the guests had been satisfied.

We did just that. I poured my tea and then topped it with more milk than I probably should have, considering the way Diana eyed me disapprovingly. I wiggled my eyebrows at her in response, and she nearly choked on her tea from laughter. We moved to the fringes of the room, where Rachel and one of Detective Grey's neighbors, Katie Glasson, sat, deep in excited conversation.

"Can we join you?" Diana asked as we reached them. Rachel sat up, nearly spilling her tea as she beamed at us.

"Of course you can! The more the merrier," she said, ignoring Katie who was asking her to be more careful.

Katie rolled her eyes playfully at Rachel and turned to us with an exasperated look.

"Hello ladies. Please sit—Rachel is driving me crazy."

Rachel gasped theatrically and shot Katie a wide eyed look. "Katie! I thought you liked my company!"

Katie rolled her eyes again. "That's not what I said. Besides, that's the *third* time in the span of ten minutes that you've nearly bathed yourself with hot tea, Rachel. You're going to give me gray hairs at this rate."

Diana sat next to Rachel, and I sat on the other side, next to Katie. Katie Glasson, like myself, was a relative newcomer to Picklesquare, having moved only five years earlier. She was a regular customer at the bakery, and Diana and I had gotten used to seeing her pop in every Monday and Tuesday for a slice of chocolate cake on her way to work at the local hospital or to drop her kids off at school.

"You guys know each other?" I asked, seconds before realizing that without clarifying it sounded like a stupid question. They were sitting next to each other and chatting like they'd been familiar with each other for quite a long time. Of course they knew each other.

Rachel just nodded. Thankfully she understood my question.

"Yeah, Katie was one of the first people I met in Picklesquare when I got here, and ever since then we've been friends."

"What she actually means," Katie cut in, "is that she latched on to me *desperately* and hasn't let go of me ever since then."

We all chuckled at that. We had to excuse ourselves minutes later, as one of the guests required more tea and didn't know where to get it. When we were done helping the elderly woman who I was sure had some form of dementia or the like, Diana and I took a pause to catch our breaths, inspecting the table and making sure everything was in order.

"Hey, look at this," Diana said, pointing at one of the only full cups on the table. I looked at it but didn't see anything out of the ordinary.

"What am I supposed to be looking at?" I asked. She huffed and picked up the cup carefully, lifting it to the level of my eyes so I could look at it properly. I stared at it in confusion for a moment before it finally clicked.

"Oh, I see—the tea in it has an amber color, while the others are just brown, right?" I said, still not understanding why it was important. Yes, the tea looked different from the other cups in the set, but that didn't require the attention Diana was giving it, right? Couldn't the color have come from the honey?

She shook her head at me. "Yes, but that's not all. Where did it come from?"

I lifted an eyebrow. "Diana, we have more important things to worry about than one cup of tea being out of place in Helena Parkson's tea party—"

Diana nodded at me knowingly. "You get it at last?"

"Where did this tea come from?" I leaned closer to inspect it more thoroughly. I had dismissed it without much thought only seconds before, yet when I thought about it properly, there was no way that honey would make the tea that color. Diana was the one who had made the tea, but I was aware that the tea Helena had used was just plain black tea, albeit expensive black tea.

Diana shrugged. "Beats me, but how about we don't leave this on the table and just throw it away instead?"

I was all for that decision, but I looked around the room before I replied. No one else looked like they were missing a cup of tea, and there were enough cups left over and enough tea in all the tea pots if anyone wanted more tea. I turned back to Diana.

"Let's trash it. Can you imagine having another death here, only this one caused by our tea? Helena would be hysterical," I said. Diana shot me a small grin as she placed her cup on the table and shifted the suspicious tea cup into her right hand. We made our way to the kitchen.

Rachel and Katie sat at the table, and Katie was telling Rachel one of her many anecdotes about her mischievous twins while Rachel took tiny bites of a pink frosted cupcake. They looked up at us when we stepped into the kitchen, and Katie grinned at us.

"Ladies. Catering duties over?"

I snorted as I joined them at the table. Diana moved over to the counter and put the cup on the countertop.

"I wish. We've gotten a little break for now, but we'll still have to tidy up after the guests have all gone."

Katie seemed surprised. "Really? I would have thought Helena would have hired someone to clean up or something – doesn't she have a housekeeper?"

Diana chimed in from behind us. "She does, and we're not going to clean the house. We just have to take our things away – mostly the trays we used for the pastries and some of the cups."

"I see." Katie nodded. Then she turned round to face Diana. "You don't like tea?"

Diana looked surprised at the question. "I do. Why would you think that?"

Katie shrugged. "You're not drinking your tea."

Diana looked down at the cup in surprise. "Oh, this?" She stepped forward and tilted the cup so we could all see the contents. "It looks a little weird, doesn't it? I wanted to throw it away."

Rachel shook her head in mock disapproval. "That's such a waste of good tea. It looks fine to me," she disagreed.

Diana frowned at the cup and hummed. "I think you might be right. It looks different now, in this lighting."

I leaned over and looked in the cup. She was right – it *did* look different. Now it just looked like regular black tea was supposed to look.

Were we seeing things? I wondered, but there was no time to ponder how odd it was that the tea looked so much different under fluorescent bulbs than in the sunlight streaming in through the windows in the living room, because just then Helena poked her head into the kitchen.

"Charlotte? Are there any more scones? People have been asking for seconds."

I grinned and slid off the stool, moving to the counter and displaying the extra box of pastries we'd brought in.

"We made extra, and luckily we brought them, just in case."

Helena's smile widened. "Well, why don't you put those on a tray and bring them out while I go tell my guests the good news?"

She left the room as soon as the last word left her mouth. Diana and I bustled about the room while Katie and Rachel talked in muted tones, sipping their tea and watching us. We took the pastries, now arranged on a large round platter, out into the living room, where the guests descended on them like a flock of birds the moment we stepped away from the table.

Of course they did it gracefully and without pushing or squawking, but it was still funny to see the way they almost queued up to get the pastries. Diana and I looked at each other.

"What now?" she asked before I could. I shrugged.

"Let's enjoy the party?"

We did just that, helping ourselves to some scones and finding an unoccupied couch to sit on while watching the guests. Diana got up after a while and went back into the kitchen, coming back out minutes later with the tea cup we'd looked at suspiciously in her hand.

"You haven't thrown it away?" I asked, raising an eyebrow at her. She shrugged.

"It looks okay, doesn't it? Like Rachel said, it would be a waste to throw away perfectly good tea just because we thought it looked weird."

I wasn't completely convinced, but it was ultimately her choice and not mine.

"If you say so, I guess."

She sat next to me and nudged my shoulder with hers.

"I *do* say so and stop worrying, would you? We're nearly done here, and all we have to do while we wait is sit and enjoy the results of our hard work. I'd say that's a plus, isn't it?"

I sighed but returned her smile, even though mine was smaller than hers. I told myself to relax, letting go of the tension in my shoulders and sinking back into the soft couch with a pleased hum. Whatever I thought about Helena, she knew what true quality was.

I turned back to Diana just in time to see her take a sip of the tea. She swallowed, a funny look on her face and then turned to me.

"Charlotte, it *does* taste funny—"

I never got to find out what the rest of her statement was, because the cup fell out of her hands and onto the velvet rug, a dark patch spreading around the cup immediately after. At the same time, Diana began to gasp for breath, and as she took in one large breath through her mouth she immediately fell to the floor, crushing the cup under her knees as a white foam escaped her lips.

I dropped the half-eaten cake in my hand without thinking and stumbled off the couch, falling on my knees beside Diana. My heart was beating so hard I thought it would burst out of my chest. I shook Diana hard as I called for help.

"Diana? Diana! Answer me!"

Somewhere deep inside I was aware that shaking her might not be the best thing to do at this time, but I had no idea what to do instead. I could feel the movements of people around me, and I was sure the warm hand on my shoulder was Katie who was saying something to me, but I couldn't hear anything.

"Diana!" I called again, but somehow I knew it was futile.

Katie confirmed what I already knew a minute later, after I'd been wrested away from Diana's body and herded into an armchair out of sight of my friend lying on the floor.

She gave me a sympathetic look, but I could see her trying to hold back her shock.

"I'm sorry, Charlotte. She's dead."

3

・ ◆ ・

DETECTIVES AGAIN

Diana is dead?

I processed this information with a sort of bodily detachment as Katie spoke to me. She told me that Diana might have had an allergic reaction to the tea. I wanted to tell her how far-fetched that was. It was more likely that she'd already had something wrong with her before any of this started, or that she'd been poisoned. But my mouth wasn't moving.

I knew which of the two possibilities I was leaning toward. *But why would anyone want to poison Diana?*

This thought of Diana being poisoned brought me back to my body, and immediately I felt the entire situation hit me again. *Diana was dead, and someone had poisoned her!*

I felt sick to my stomach at the thought of it, and I had to swallow to keep the hot ball of bile in my throat down. All I wanted to do right now was curl up and cry. My heart hurt so much that it felt like someone had gouged out the piece of my heart I'd set aside for Diana.

I wanted to go home, draw all the curtains, curl up in my bed, and stay there until someone told me Diana was alive, and it was all just a prank.

I couldn't do that though. Couldn't cry like I wanted to, or just shut down even though I was already so tired, because Helena Parkson was walking my way, and I had to say something to her.

Never mind that I didn't have the strength to deal with whatever she would say, especially since I suspected I wasn't going to like it.

"Charlotte! What is going on?" the words were halfway out of her mouth before her eyes widened, and I guessed she'd finally caught sight of Diana's body crumpled up on the carpet. She quickly softened her tone, looking at Katie and thankfully leaving me alone.

"Oh–I had no idea. What happened?"

Katie shook her head. "I'm not sure, but she suddenly foamed at the mouth and fell to the floor—"

"That's not what happened," I cut in sharply. Katie flinched at my tone, but I was past the point of caring about social niceties.

Helena held up a hand before I could continue. "Why don't we take this outside, into the gazebo? It's quiet there, and we can call the police when you've told me everything."

I agreed without much thought, though the cynical part of me sneered that Helena was only acting kind and the real reason she wanted us outside was so there would be no gossip about her if she was implicated in some way. The other part said I was being silly and to just be grateful for the kindness I'd been given.

Helena led us out through a side door adjacent to the kitchen, apologizing to the guests as we went but politely kicking them out. I walked ahead of them, going over to the gazebo that loomed in the distance. Behind me I could hear Helena calling someone named Ingrid and asking the person to cover the body.

The body, I repeated in my mind. That was all Diana was now. Just a bag of cooling blood, flesh and bones. I stopped in the middle of the pathway leading up to the gazebo and covered my mouth, squeezing my eyes tightly until the heat behind my eyes receded and the urge to break out into maniacal laughter died down.

There was a hand on my shoulder. The scent of baby powder told me it was Katie.

"Are you feeling alright, Charlotte?"

Can I truly be alright with what's happened to me? I wanted to ask. It wouldn't be fair to her though—she clearly knew I wasn't alright mentally. She was asking about my physical well being.

I nodded. "I'm okay," I managed to force out. She didn't look like she believed me, but I was grateful that she didn't press me about it and instead led me into the gazebo after taking my hand.

Rachel was already seated in the gazebo when we arrived, and I pushed down the urge to glare at her, wishing looks could kill. She was the one who had convinced Diana the tea was safe to drink—but I was being unreasonable. Diana had chosen to drink it when Rachel wasn't even there, and it wasn't fair to blame her, even though I desperately needed someone to direct my anger at.

We sat in the gazebo, waiting for Helena to come out. I wondered what Rachel was doing out here, but I didn't care enough to ask. The atmosphere was awkward, most likely because of me, and when Helena finally made her way up to us, sitting beside Rachel, the tension in the air eased and it felt like we could breathe a little easier.

"Now will someone tell me what has happened? And I'm sorry for your loss, Charlotte. I know Diana was a dear friend to you," Helena said. I nodded at her. She was being sincere, and I knew it was because she knew how it felt to lose a loved one.

Katie looked at me. I sighed and began to tell the story.

"There's nothing much to say, really. I guess where it all started was when Diana noticed the cup of tea on the table. It didn't look like actual tea—it had this amber color that we thought was honey at first. We took it back to the kitchen to throw it away, but it looked different and normal, so she must have thought that it would be okay, and maybe it was just the light that made it look different."

I stopped and took in a deep breath, willing myself not to cry. Katie rubbed my arm and whispered that it was alright, and to take as much time as I needed to. I shook my head and composed myself.

"I'm fine Katie, really. Where was I? Oh, yes, the tea. Anyway after that, she took a sip, and she sort of stiffened. The cup fell out of her hand and then she fell too. Then she started foaming at the mouth and well... that was it," I finished abruptly, leaving a heavy silence behind.

"I'm really sorry about this, Charlotte," Helena finally said.

I shrugged. "Thank you, but it wasn't your fault."

Her eyes narrowed. "What do you mean by that?"

Katie answered for me, which was just as well, because I was too angry to hold myself from spitting out all the rage I held inside me.

"Charlotte thinks Diana's tea was poisoned."

Helena and Rachel leaned back, as if the words had hit them physically. Helena found my gaze, searching my face for something. Whatever she was looking for she didn't find, because she shook her head.

"Charlotte, I know that you're angry, but you can't just leap to wild conclusions—"

"Thank you for the advice, Helena," I cut her off. "But I'll take it from here. Sorry about ruining your party."

I stood up and walked out of the gazebo. I felt smothered and still deeply shocked by what had happened. Katie came after me.

"Charlotte, where are you going?"

I looked over my shoulder at her. "Don't worry. I'm not going far. I'm just going to call Detective Grey and the police, if they haven't done that already." I gestured with my head at the house to indicate who the "they" I was speaking about was. She still looked concerned for me, but in the end she nodded and let me go.

I had Detective Grey on speed dial, so I stopped in the middle of the pathway to call him.

"Charlotte? This is a surprise. What's up?"

His voice sounded bright, even for him, and I felt even sadder that I was about to ruin his day. I sniffed—when did I start crying?—and forced the words out.

"Diana's dead. Please come to Helena Parkson's house."

I ended the call immediately. I didn't have the strength to entertain any questions. All I wanted right now was to put the bastard who had killed my best friend behind bars. Now that I'd called Detective Grey, what was next? I didn't want to go back to the gazebo and face all the pitying looks from everyone, but I also didn't want to go back into the house to wait for Detective Grey. I could see that most of the guests were still around even though Helena had ended the party. It sickened me to see how they whispered to each other as if it was just regular juicy gossip and not someone's death that had happened.

I eventually decided to go hole up in the kitchen. The only people I might run into were Helena's housekeeper and probably the cleaning staff, but they might have the decency to leave me alone. Also I needed to pack up the things we'd brought to the house, even if Diana was no longer here to help me with it.

I entered the house just as the police arrived with an ambulance in tow, sirens blaring and making everything even more noisy and confusing. I tried to escape into the kitchen, but one of the officers

- Officer Larson, I vaguely remember her introducing herself to me - tracked me down and asked me to give a statement while the paramedics took Diana's body away and the rest of the cops secured the crime scene and gathered the evidence.

She was nice enough to let me choose the location, and luckily the kitchen was free. I told her exactly what I'd told Helena, Katie, and Rachel. The officer seemed almost disappointed there wasn't more of the story, but made up for it by asking questions. Who made the tea? Had Diana put her cup down anywhere? Who was with us in the kitchen and at the table? Did we notice anyone acting suspicious? Did Diana have any enemies or rivals?

Most of my answers were negative, and I was starting to feel frustrated. I couldn't see any reason for anyone to poison Diana, and it seemed the police didn't either. The officer shut her notepad and was giving me a little speech about what was going to happen next when Detective Bush poked his head through the doorway.

"Charlotte, Larson," he said, nodding at the woman and coming into the room. "Are you done here?"

Officer Larson frowned at him, but nodded.

"Please excuse us then."

She did as he asked, and immediately after she was out the door he came over and gave me a hug. When he finally let go, he looked at me and sighed.

"I know how important Diana was to you, so I'm not even going to bother asking if you're alright. Do you want me to drive you home? Detective Grey will be here soon."

I shook my head. "No. I want to stay. I want to know what's going on."

He nodded. "I'll let you know if we've found anything."

I thanked him, my voice low, and he stepped back out. I put my forearms on the table and placed my head on them, head turned towards the right. I closed my eyes.

The next time I opened them Detective Grey sat across from me. He gave me a sad, sympathetic look when I met his eyes. I looked away. I didn't want to see the pity on his face just then.

"How long was I out for?"

"Nearly three hours."

I looked out the window. The sun had gone down, and the house was quieter than before. Only muted conversation from outside could be heard. I turned back to him.

"And?" I said. "Have you gotten anything?"

He sighed. "I'm not on the case, but Detective Bush is. And from what he told me, none of the guests had done anything but pour the tea into their cups. They all left the table after that, and everyone was watching each other, so no one saw anyone tamper with the tea. The only ones who had the opportunity were you and Diana."

My face crumpled, and he quickly spoke. "They did a test on her blood though—the poison worked so fast that it was already in her bloodstream the second she drank it."

"They know what it is?" I said hopefully.

For some reason, he sighed at my question. Whatever he told me next, I knew I wasn't going to like it.

"They do, after many tests and a lot of deliberation. They don't know what it is or what it's called, but they're referencing an old alchemical textbook written nearly five hundred years ago that describes this exact same situation. According to the experts, it's rare and there have only been about ten sightings of it throughout history—Charlotte?"

I laid my head down on my forearms and sobbed into my arms. It hurt to think that even if Diana had somehow hung on to life until we'd gotten her to the hospital, she would have still died anyway.

4

RIDDLES AND REVIVAL

One day after my life had been turned upside down by my best friend's death by an ancient poison, I sat at my kitchen table, taking large gulps out of a mug of coffee Detective Grey had handed to me when I stepped into the kitchen.

I didn't even want to know how he had gotten into the house. I didn't care, which was dangerous, but at that point I was done with everything.

"Slow down, Charlotte," Detective Grey said, concern evident in his voice.

I frowned into my coffee. I didn't know what to say to him, especially since he looked as haggard as I felt.

"Did you even sleep?" I asked. Just at that moment Pearl strutted in through the kitchen door and leapt onto the table, settling in the center without even knocking anything off.

Detective Grey stroked her until she shifted. That was his cue to stop petting her. I narrowed my eyes at him.

"Did you sleep?" I repeated slowly. I wasn't one to talk, seeing as I had barely slept myself. I kept waking up and walking to Diana's room to check if she was there. She never was. Somehow I slept in the wee hours of the morning, waking up to the sun's rays in my eyes.

"About as well as you did," was his answer. I glared at him.

"So you didn't sleep then?"

"And it seems you didn't either," he retorted, but there was no heat in it.

I sighed, suddenly bone-tired. I put down the nearly empty mug and got to my feet.

"Do you want something to eat?" I asked, walking to the fridge and opening it to look in. The fridge was fully stocked, courtesy of my now dead friend. The hardest thing about Diana's death was the giant hole she'd left in my life–our lives. Diana was everywhere I looked: it was her apron on the hook behind the door, as I had never gotten into the habit of using aprons. Her baking stuff was still in the sink: I hadn't felt like washing them the night before and had just thrown them in the sink.

When he didn't answer, I looked over my shoulder at him.

"Hello? Anyone home?"

He was staring into thin air, just past the spot where I'd been sitting, but at my words he shook his head.

"What? No, no food for me, thanks."

I frowned at him. "Did you eat before getting here?"

He nodded. "My dad made sure," he said. I shrugged and plucked a plate of leftover food out of the fridge and carried it over to the microwave. After putting it in and setting the timer, I returned to the table.

"So what's next?"

Detective Grey sighed. "We haven't gotten any leads on the case—"

My phone rang, and I held up a hand. "Sorry, I should probably take this—an unknown caller?"

I paused and looked at him. "Do I answer?"

He shrugged. "Why not?"

So I picked up the call.

"Charlotte Miller?" a heavily modulated voice said. I looked at Detective Grey again, furrowing my brows.

"That's me," I replied slowly. "Who is this?"

"Put it on speaker," Detective Grey mouthed. I took the phone away from my ear and set it down on the table between us, moving Pearl to the side to make space for it. Then I put the call on speaker mode.

"That's not important right now—"

I frowned at the phone and cut in, "Excuse me, but I think it *is* important. I can't trust you if I don't know who you are and what you want from me."

The voice laughed. It was not a pleasant sound. It grated on my ears like chalk being dragged down a blackboard, and I fought the urge to cover my ears.

"You don't need to trust me, Charlotte. You want something, and I can give it to you."

I exchanged looks with Detective Grey. He looked concerned but didn't signal me to end the phone call, so I leaned in and responded.

"And what is it that you think I want?"

The laughter came again. I was starting to feel a murderous urge toward this person.

"You mean to tell me you don't want your dear Diana back?"

My heart stopped, and moments later I realized I wasn't breathing.

"This is not funny," I said through gritted teeth, clenching my jaw so hard that it started to hurt.

"I was laughing before, but I can assure you, Charlotte, I am serious. I know a way to bring her back to life."

Detective Grey was shaking his head violently, and he even reached out for the phone. I snatched it up before he got to it and stepped back from the table, eyeing him warily.

"*Charlotte!*" he hissed. "Don't fall for whatever this is—"

"And what do you want in return? I'm not gullible enough to think you're just going to bring Diana back for free."

The voice chuckled. "Smart girl. There's a certain object under the Parkson's mansion—if I'm not mistaken, you already know about it."

My heart dropped into my stomach. I turned around and looked at Detective Grey, who was now on his feet, arms folded and glaring at me. I realized he wasn't going to offer any suggestions besides telling me to cut the call, so I turned back to the call and said the best thing I could think of.

"What object? I have no idea what you're talking about," I lied, hoping against all hope that this person wasn't referring to the Dark Stone.

"Oh please," the person scoffed. "Don't play dumb. I'll humor you though. I'm speaking about the Dark Stone. Does that ring a bell?"

I shook my head, then realized whoever it was couldn't see me—at least I hoped they couldn't.

"I've never heard anything like that before now," I persisted.

"Whatever you say, Charlotte. Just get me the stone, and dear Diana will be back with you, smiling like she never left."

With those words the call ended. The next moment there was a chime from my phone, indicating I had a text. I was about to swipe the notification away when I noticed it was from the same number that had called me.

"I got a text," I said to Detective Grey, who was still glaring at me like it was going to make me apologize. When he realized I was going to do what I wanted whether he supported me or not, he sighed and walked over to me.

"What does it say?"

I shook my head and passed the phone to him. It was a short paragraph, reading like a poem. At the end of the text, on a new line, were the words: *The key to the maze is in these words. Do it for Diana.*

"It's a riddle then," Detective Grey said. "Hey, where are you going?"

I was halfway out the kitchen door, and I didn't stop as I made my way up the stairs and back to my room.

"I'm going to take a quick shower and change into something appropriate," I called back.

"Charlotte!" I heard his footsteps follow me out of the kitchen, but by the time he got to the foot of the stairs the door of my room was closing behind me.

I knew it was foolish to believe completely in the strange person who wanted the Dark Stone, but I couldn't pass up a chance to revive Diana, even as suspicious as it sounded and felt. I hopped into the shower and was out in five minutes, changing into an old flannel shirt and my heavy-duty jeans before throwing on my old hiking boots. I grabbed my bag, which I hadn't unpacked from Diana's death day and hurried down the stairs.

Detective Grey sat in the living room, Pearl on his lap. He looked up at me and frowned.

"And where are you going?"

I shot him an annoyed look. "To the maze, of course! Where else would I be going?"

He sighed. "Charlotte—"

I interrupted him before he could try to dissuade me. "I know what you're going to say. Believe me, I've already thought of everything you've thought of. But what's the alternative—sitting here and moping around? At least even if this person isn't legit I'll have the Dark Stone."

"And if they are?"

I shrugged, not meeting his eyes. "We'll cross that bridge when we come to it. Now are you coming with me or not?"

He huffed, but got to his feet, carrying Pearl in his arms as we walked to the door.

"Are we bringing Pearl with us?" I asked.

He raised an eyebrow at me. "Are we not?"

I shrugged. "I guess? She's been a real help, so it makes sense to have her come along this time, too."

We locked the door behind us and got into Detective Grey's car, and we were off. On the way to the Parkson's mansion, I read the riddle again.

"' Blood now cold, stiff in his hold, my limbs don't work anymore.' What does that even mean?"

"Death?" Detective Grey guessed.

"A corpse?" I shook my head. "It's something to do with death, all right, but we won't know for sure until we get into the maze."

We drove the rest of the way in silence, lost in our own thoughts and grief. We were supposed to comfort each other, but instead, we'd pushed down our grief and threw ourselves into work. It wasn't exactly healthy, but I was sure Detective Grey didn't care, and I didn't either. I would rather work myself into burnout than do the healthy thing and mourn properly.

We finally arrived at the mansion. Helena had left town for a while on a cruise, claiming she didn't want to deal with the stress and the police presence in her house. I sympathized with her, but I couldn't help being glad she wasn't around to watch us traipse around under her house. It was even better that we didn't have to explain exactly why we were in the maze or what we wanted the Dark Stone for.

When we parked in the driveway and got out of the car Detective Bush was already standing there, waiting for us.

"Charlotte, Grey," he nodded at us as we walked up to him. "What are you doing here?"

"We need to go down into the maze," I said.

He raised an eyebrow at me. "For the Dark Stone? No offense, Charlotte, but I doubt that either of you are in the right frame of mind to conduct that search right now."

I scowled at him. "It's not just the Dark Stone, Detective Bush. It's—" I looked around us. There were other cops around, but none of them were in hearing range.

"Charlotte?" he said, eyeing me in confusion. Then he turned to his colleague. "What is she doing?"

Detective Grey looked faintly amused. "She's checking that there's no one eavesdropping. She's about to say something that might make her sound crazy, that's why."

I ignored him, rolling my eyes. I leaned towards Detective Bush and told him about the call I'd gotten and the deal we'd made. He looked as disapproving as Detective Grey was, but neither of them stopped me from walking to the garden and towards the entrance of the maze.

The door to the maze was far behind the house, and as we got closer to the door the more unkempt the grounds became, such that by the time we stood in front of the door we were knee-deep in a sea of grass. The door was less like a door and more like a wall because there was no visible handle on it. Instead, there were two bronze statues on square bases on either side of the door. The left one was a horse rearing back and the right one was a lion, roaring at the viewer.

On the surface of the stone bases of the statues, just by the hooves of the horse, a small rectangle with words in it was etched in the stone. It read: "Speak and enter."

"I'm guessing this means we have to say the answer to the riddle out loud?" I mused. The men nodded, and we took turns telling our answers to the horse, and then to the lion. Nothing worked. I was about to tear my hair out from frustration when I heard a cheery voice behind us.

"Hello? Are you guys trying to get into the maze?"

We turned around at the same time and watched Rachel wade through the grass to join us.

"Rachel? What are you still doing here?"

She shrugged and smiled at me. "Someone had to take care of the house, and Helena jumped at the opportunity when I offered, so here I am. You're trying to get into the maze, right? I can help."

Detectives Grey and Bush looked at me as if asking what to do. I still didn't like her very much, but I shrugged and stepped aside. My feelings about her didn't matter if she helped us achieve our goal.

She stepped in between the statues, and asked aloud, "Horse, Lion, what is the answer to the riddle?"

"Is she serious?" Detective Bush asked in a low whisper. Detective Grey didn't say anything, but I could see the skepticism on his face. I hadn't told him about Rachel's abilities, but it didn't matter, because the horse *moved* its mouth and said in a thick, gravelly voice that felt like it was speaking in capital letters, "Rigor."

Then the lion opened its mouth as well and said in the same voice, "Mortis."

Rachel turned to us, beaming, and winked at us. She faced the door again and said in a loud voice, "Rigor mortis."

The door to the maze slid to the side smoothly, leaving the rest of us, apart from Rachel, gaping.

5

PREPARATIONS

We were back in the mansion, Rachel having let us in and avoiding the police tape. The officers around us eyed us but said nothing as we passed. I wondered what Detective Bush had told them, since he was in charge, but ultimately I didn't care. All I cared about was getting down into that maze and getting the Dark Stone, and as long as they did their job of catching Diana's killer and I did mine, why would I care?

There was also the added annoyance of Rachel tagging along on our quest for the Dark Stone. We'd basically exchanged her help with the door to the maze with letting her come along, but I couldn't help being annoyed at how easily the two detectives had accepted her excuse of being bored being alone in the house when I'd asked why she wanted to come along.

It wasn't that I didn't trust her, but I couldn't help blaming her for Diana's decision to drink the poisoned tea. It made no sense, but emotions had never been logical in the first place. She must have felt my dislike for her because she kept her words to a minimum around me and only spoke to me when it was necessary. Somehow that made me even more annoyed with her.

"So when are we going down?" Detective Grey asked as we sat around the kitchen table. Daya Grant and her boyfriend, John Garrison, had come to join us, and were listening intently.

"It has to be soon," I replied, chewing on my lip as I thought. "If we wait any longer we might not be allowed in the house anymore, right?" I asked, looking at Detective Bush for confirmation.

He furrowed his brows, thinking, but nodded after a while. "It'll start to look suspicious if you show up while the investigation is still going on and then ask to go into the maze, and you might not get permission. Best to do it now while things are still settling down."

I nodded. "Just as I thought. Can we go right now?"

Detective Grey leaned back to give me a dubious look. "Now? Charlotte, we're not ready."

"And we might never be. How do we even prepare for whatever is in there? For all we know, it's just a maze, and all we need might just be something to lead us in and out, like a ball of yarn."

He sighed, but accepted that there was no stopping me.

"I'll go and get some stuff to help us, I guess," he said, getting up and walking out. Rachel looked at me.

"Do I need to bring anything?" she asked.

I shrugged and shook my head. "You can bring whatever you want, but like I said to Detective Grey, I don't know. Just bring whatever you think might help us."

She grinned and got up, leaving the kitchen in a breeze. Detective Bush looked at me.

"You're not taking anything?"

I lifted my bag to show it to him. "I have my stuff here, and I guess Detective Grey will bring enough stuff for both of us."

I stopped, and pointed at Pearl, sitting on the windowsill and enjoying the warm morning sun. "And I have Pearl too. I think that's more than enough."

That forced a tiny grin out of him, and he nodded and turned to Daya and John. "And why are you two here?"

Daya looked at me. I shrugged back. *I didn't know why she was here either.*

"Detective Grey called me and asked me to come. John was with me, so he decided to tag along. I hope that's fine?"

Detective Bush and I nodded at the same time.

"He must have called you here for a reason. I guess we'll know when he gets back," I said. She gave me a small smile and went back to whispering with her boyfriend. They were cute together, and watching them made me smile for the first time in two days.

Just then, Detective Grey burst back into the kitchen, an army green backpack slung over one shoulder. It looked like it had seen much better days, but was somehow still holding on.

"You're back in what, two minutes?" Detective Bush said, raising an eyebrow at his colleague. "That was suspiciously fast."

Detective Grey brushed it off. "I always keep a bag on hand in my car."

"That's not suspicious at all," Detective Bush said.

Detective Grey just raised an eyebrow at him.

"What can I say? I like to be prepared, that's all. There are flashlights in there—I'll give you one when we get into the maze, and I brought walkie-talkies in case our phones die. I also brought—"

"You *are* prepared," Detective Bush said, wonder in his voice. "Do you walk around expecting to go on adventures or something?"

Detective Grey smiled. He never answered the question though, because just then Rachel came back into the room. She also had a backpack over her shoulders, but hers was much smaller than Detective Grey's and she'd changed into cargo pants, with a dark denim jacket over her t-shirt.

"I'm ready," she said. "When are we setting off?"

Detective Grey shook his head. "Not yet. Sit. We still have some things to hash out."

Rachel looked at me for confirmation, seemingly puzzled, but I was as clueless as she was. I shrugged and she repeated the action, taking her former stool. When she was finally settled we looked back at Detective Grey, and Daya and John sat at attention.

"So here's what we're going to do: Charlotte, Rachel, and I are going to go down into the maze—" Pearl meowed loudly from the window, and we laughed. "—and Pearl, of course, will go with us, while the three of you will stay up here."

"And what are we going to be doing?" Daya asked.

"Well, the tests revealed the poison, and we've declined an autopsy. So Diana's body will be back here this afternoon, and I want you two here watching over it." He paused. "Sorry, I'm giving you such a morbid job."

John nodded. "I don't mind. It's not like we have to sit next to her body all the time. You just want us to watch over it, right?"

Detective Grey looked at Daya. "Are you fine with that, Daya?" he asked.

She shivered and then sat up straighter. "Sure. Like John said, it's not a big deal. I kind of had to do the same when my grandma died, so I'm fine with it. Why do you need *us* to watch over the body though? The police have basically occupied this house anyway, and Detective Bush is here too."

I looked at him. "Yeah, why?"

I don't see any reason why Daya and John might be a better choice for the task of guarding Diana's body, and I don't see why they had to have that responsibility in the first place.

"What if the killer comes back? We don't know why they targeted Diana out of everyone who was here that day, and we don't know if they'll be back for whatever reason. I think it's best to keep her body under watch until we can bury her or," he glanced at me, "until we get her back."

Daya and John looked puzzled, but they didn't ask. Rachel just kept smiling, like she was happy to be here no matter how morbid the topic of discussion had turned out to be.

"And I'll be busy trying to track down the killer before they poison anyone again with the rare and fatal poison," Detective Bush added. "Or before they can get to the Dark Stone," he amended immediately.

"Is that all?" I asked after a moment, looking around the table. Detective Grey nodded, and when no one else seemed to have anything to say, I got to my feet.

"Well, if that's all, let's go. There's no time to waste," I announced.

Detective Grey and Rachel stood up too, carrying their bags. We left the kitchen through the back door and wasted no time making our way to the maze, Pearl walking right beside us and disappearing in the grass at times.

The door was still open when we arrived, but from the untouched dust on the floor, it was clear no one had gone in before us. Pearl stepped into the doorway and looked up at us, meowing softly.

"Pearl? What is it?" I asked. She meowed again and then began to glow.

Detective Grey and I looked at each other with wide eyes. What was she going to do now? I suddenly remembered that Rachel was with us, and when I glanced at her she was looking back at me with equally wide eyes.

"Your cat is glowing," she said.

I shrugged, a small smile on my face. I was proud of Pearl, for some reason.

"She does that sometimes," I said. Just as the glow died down, a figure stepped out of the doorway from behind Pearl. My eyes widened and I gasped when I saw who it was.

"Diana? I thought you were dead!"

As she stepped forward, my shoulders slumped when I took her in properly. She was nearly transparent in the sunlight, and only when she stepped back into the darkness beyond the doorway could we see her properly.

"You're a ghost now?" I whispered. She nodded, giving me a sad smile, and I clenched my fist, my nails digging into my palms.

"You can't speak?" Detective Grey asked suddenly. He looked as calm as ever, but I could see the subtle hints in his face that said he wasn't as unruffled as he tried to look. Rachel, for her part, just looked between all of us with wide eyes.

Diana's ghost shook her head. I sighed and looked at my cat. "Is she coming with us?"

Pearl meowed and licked her paw. Rachel looked between us frantically.

"You guys look so calm. Is this normal for you two?"

No one answered her.

What could we say that wouldn't scare a sane person?

6

LABYRINTH

Rachel never got an answer though.

Pearl meowed and walked quickly into the darkness ahead of us. We looked at each other, and when Diana's ghost floated after her we knew instinctively that we had to go in after them.

Detective Grey fished his flashlight out of the side pocket of his backpack and switched it on, pointing it into the dark corridor. The ray of light pierced through the dark and showed us a small glimpse of what we would be walking into in a few seconds.

The walls and the floor were blanketed with dust, and cobwebs hung low from the ceiling and corners. I could already feel the sneeze somewhere in the back of my nose threatening to leave my nose. I rubbed my nose, scrunching it up.

"You okay?" Detective Grey asked, nudging my arm with an elbow.

I nodded and rubbed my nose again. "I'll be fine. I just have to get used to it."

Rachel stepped forward, turning on the flashlight of her phone.

"This is kind of creepy, but it's also exciting." She paused and looked over her shoulder at us.

"Are you guys coming or not?"

"We're coming," I replied, stepping into the darkness after her. I could feel the warmth of Detective Grey's presence close behind me, and it made me feel a bit safer and more comfortable as we walked into the unknown ahead of us. I could hear the clicking of Pearl's claws on the stone floor some distance ahead of us, but even peering over Rachel's shoulder didn't show me where she was.

"Where are we going?" Rachel asked after a while. "Do we just keep going forward, or...?" She trailed off, turning her head to me slightly.

I shook my head. "I have no idea. I know that the Dark Stone is at the center of the maze, but we don't know *how* to get there. I guess we just keep going until we get to the center—what's that?"

Detective Grey shone his light in the direction where I was pointing, some distance ahead of us to our left, and the light stopped on a brown rectangular part of the wall that turned into an arch at the top. We quickly walked up to it and Rachel traced her fingers along it, making neat lines in the dust that covered the brown material we could now see was polished wood.

"It looks like a door, but there's no doorknob," she said. I leaned in to get a better look at it and gingerly wiped off some dust, leaving a clean square behind. There were crimson lines painted on the wood, and I looked back at my companions.

"Does anyone have a cloth or a handkerchief they'd like to donate to our cause?" I said.

Rachel thought for a moment.

"I have some tissue if you want," she said, digging into the pocket of her jacket and bringing out a wad of folded tissues. I took them from her with a thankful nod and turned back to the door, wiping the dust from the entire door while Detective Grey and Rachel watched.

When I was sure there was no more dust on the door I balled up the now dirty tissues in my fist and stepped back to take in the door properly. Rachel and Detective Grey aimed their lights at the door, and Rachel let out a quiet gasp beside me.

The painted lines I'd seen had only been a tiny part of an entire picture that covered the door. It was a large drawing of a tree whose branches seemed to reach out beyond the edges of the door like they would grow onto the walls around the door if they could.

"Does it mean anything?" Detective Grey said, frowning at the door.

I shrugged. "I have no idea, but don't you think it might be significant somehow?"

I felt rather than saw him shaking his head on my other side. "It might be significant some other time, but right now our priority is bringing Diana back. And giving away the Dark Stone, of course."

I turned to him, feeling incredulous. *Is he really still mad that I accepted my unknown caller's deal?*

"You didn't have to come with me, you know," I said, doing my best to hold back the annoyance I had every right to feel. He could have just stayed with Detective Bush back in the house if he wasn't going to be helpful. A second later, I mentally shook my head at my thoughts. *He has been helpful, and he came to help me even if he still doesn't approve of what I am doing. I don't have to antagonize him for being a good friend.*

"I didn't," he agreed, his tone mild so I couldn't tell if I'd annoyed him with my words, "but I'm not just doing this for you, you know."

He gestured with his flashlight ahead of us where Diana floated beside Pearl a few feet away. A pang of guilt hit me and I turned away from him. Diana had been his friend too, even if they hadn't been as close as Diana and I had been.

I started to apologize, but he just went on speaking. "Besides, it's not about that. If the door was important Pearl would have been scratching at the door already."

My eyes widened, and I spun around to look at my cat again. She sat in the middle of the corridor, bathing herself, and I could swear she was waiting for us to catch up with her before she would keep going.

Rachel touched the door again. Her expression was shadowed, thanks to the sparse light in the corridor, but she seemed a little irritated.

"Are you sure? No offense to the cat but *I* think this door is important," she said, running her pointer finger up along the trunk of the tree.

"Aren't you an animal whisperer?" I asked, turning to her. "You should be the one telling us what Pearl is thinking."

She shrugged and dropped her fingers. "I should, but she hasn't said anything."

"Then we'll follow Pearl?" I said. "We can always come back to the door if we need to."

There was no disagreement with my statement, so we walked up to Pearl, who spun on her feet as soon as we got to her and padded down the corridor. We followed quickly, Rachel wondering aloud where we were going in what she thought was a whisper. She grew quiet when no one answered.

The corridor seemed to go on forever. We'd been walking in a straight line for nearly ten minutes or more, and there was still no sign of a corner or any other door, like the one with the tree. I was starting to wonder if Rachel had been right after all, and we should have just gone through the door when Pearl stopped in the middle of the corridor.

"Pearl? What is it?" I asked, stepping around Detective Grey to make my way to the front. Diana's ghost floated beside the cat, and when she caught my gaze she pointed at me—rather, at the wall behind me. I turned sideways and looked at the wall.

"There's nothing there," Rachel said, coming up to me to peer at the walls, her nose almost hitting the stone. I wondered why she was doing that—her eyesight seemed fine when I'd met her, and she was pointing her light at the stone, so it wasn't like she couldn't see. Luckily Detective Grey spoke the words I'd been thinking of.

"Did you leave your contacts behind?"

Rachel turned to him with furrowed brows. "What? I don't wear contacts or glasses—my vision is 20/20."

He gestured with his flashlight at the wall. "Then why do you keep doing that—getting so close to the walls like you can't see?"

She looked stunned for a mere second, then her face cleared of confusion and she chuckled. "Oh, that. It's nothing really, I'm just checking whether there are any other markings like the one we saw on that door over there."

I narrowed my eyes at her. I felt like she was lying, but what exactly was she lying about? I let it go for the moment. There were more important things to consider. I turned to Pearl.

"Pearl, what did you want to show me?"

The cat gave me a look of disappointment if I could call it that, and begrudgingly got off her butt, walking to the wall and patting it with her left paw. I tried touching the same spot she'd touched, but nothing happened. I got a look of disdain from my cat, who went back to her spot in the middle of the corridor and lay down, closing her eyes.

"Well, does anyone else have any ideas?" I said, turning to my other companions. All Rachel did was tilt her head to the side and point at the wall again. Detective Grey kept on examining the wall with squinted eyes. Rachel frowned and stepped back.

"Beats me," she said. I sighed and turned back to the wall. What was so special about it? I inspected it again. It was the same as the other walls, dark gray, smooth except for the hair-thin, jagged line that zigzagged down the wall from the top and stopped at three-quarters of the wall—

"I think I found something!" I blurted out, practically pushing Rachel aside in my hurry to get closer. I mumbled an apology when she let out an indignant noise, but my heart wasn't in it.

"What did you find?" Detective Grey asked as I brought my fingers to the wall and gently traced the line from where it started close to me and upwards. I turned to him, took his hand, and pressed his fingers to the line.

"What do you feel?" I asked, doing my best to tamp down the excitement I felt. What if I'd just been convincing myself that I'd found something in the hopes of finally moving forward?

He frowned and pushed his fingers against the line.

"It... it feels almost as if there's a space behind the line—how do I put it—like if I had nails I could just—" He cut himself off and turned to Rachel and me.

"Which one of you has the longer nails?" he demanded. Rachel and I looked at each other, equally bemused looks on our faces. How was that information useful?

We obliged him though, and brought our hands together, palms down, to compare. Rachel's nails were better kept and longer than mine, and he ushered her forward, stepping back and giving instructions all the while.

"Can you see that line? Good. Run your nails across it and try to dig in with them, if you can."

Rachel rolled her eyes at him over her shoulder. "This is stupid, and I'm going to break my nails for nothing," she said, but she obeyed, doing exactly as he asked.

The moment she dug her nails in, there was a loud crack, and Rachel jumped back.

"What was that?" she nearly screamed, looking around wildly. There was nothing out of the ordinary that we could see, but I was still uneasy. Pearl was still on the floor, looking like she was well on her way to a nice nap.

I turned back to Rachel to reassure her, but just then we heard the crack again, and immediately after that, an even louder grinding noise from the wall we'd been staring at for the past ten minutes.

"What—" Rachel started to say, just as the line extended down to the floor.

Then the walls opened, sliding sideways and apart from each other to reveal a thin, dark corridor. We looked at each other in amazement. Detective Grey stepped through first, lighting the way for us.

The passageway was narrow, so small that ahead of me I could see Detective Grey hunching his broad shoulders just to get by, and it made me feel claustrophobic for the first time in my life. I felt like the walls would slide together again and crush us to a bloody pulp, and if we all walked faster than usual nobody minded.

We stepped out into another corridor, much like the one we'd been following before entering the passage in the walls, and it actually was the corridor we'd been in, as evidenced by the same door in front of us.

Rachel stared at the door for a moment and turned to me, a triumphant grin on her face.

"Ha! I told you it was important, didn't I?"

I was about to say something dramatic, but just then the grinding noise started again, and we turned around just in time to see the walls close behind us. When we turned back to the door it was lit up in green lines where there'd only been a dark red hue before.

I turned to Rachel and smirked. She just muttered something I didn't catch.

"Are we going in?" Detective Grey asked Pearl. The cat strode up to the door and pushed it. We watched as it opened inwards, and my mouth fell open at the sight beyond the door.

7

BOBO THE MONKEY

Trees planted in rich loamy soil were spread out before us, grass cut short on the ground just beyond the door. The sounds of wildlife greeted us from the other side of the door.

Rachel leaned closer to me, whispering, "Are you seeing what I'm seeing?"

I nodded, my mouth dry. I'd seen strange things, too many recently, in fact, but I'd never heard of a door that led to a forest. "Are we going in there?" I asked, when I finally found my voice again.

Pearl flicked my calf with her tail and stepped through the door. We looked at each other. Diana went next, and I shook my head.

"It seems like there's only one thing to do," I said, and the others nodded in agreement. I took a deep breath in, closed my eyes, let it out again and opened my eyes.

"Right," I said. "I'm ready. Let's go."

We stepped through the door after Pearl, one by one, and the door immediately snapped shut behind us. I looked back quickly, but there was only a tree where the door had just been. Rachel went further, stepping around the tree to see if there was something hidden behind it, but she shook her head after re-emerging. No luck there.

It was interesting that the bark of the tree seemed to be quite similar to the door in color, and that gave me an idea. What if the door wasn't missing mysteriously, but was just concealed in the tree? Unfortunately, minutes of poking and prodding at the tree trunk didn't reveal anything, and Rachel and I were forced to step back and admit that the door was indeed gone.

Detective Grey shook his head at us. "Nothing else to do but move on," he said.

"How are we going to get out though?" Rachel asked. "While being in a maze one moment and in a tropical rainforest the next is the most exciting thing that has happened to me recently, I'd like to be able to go home again at some point."

His only answer was a short shaking of his head. She threw up her hands, exasperation on her face and turned to me.

"Do you have a plan, Charlotte?"

I mentally frowned. *She was the one who wanted to come along, so I don't see why you're complaining now...*

"I don't, but hopefully Pearl isn't leading us astray," I said, looking past her at my cat, who was getting farther away with every second and would soon disappear among the trees if we didn't catch up. "Let's go," I continued, walking past Rachel. Detective Grey followed, falling in step with me, and I heard a huff from behind us and then footsteps.

"Are you sure we're going the right way?" Rachel called out. I looked over my shoulder at her.

"I have no idea, but let's just stick close behind Pearl and hope for the best." The last few words came out as a question instead of a reassuring statement, and it was obvious even I didn't know what I was doing. No one called me out on it though, and we spent some time trudging through the forest in silence.

It was more of a silence on the part of our group than actual silence. The sounds of nature filled the air: birds chirping and calling out to each other from above us, the rustle of leaves and grass as some small creature darted past, the rustle of the foliage high above our heads. It was beautiful too, green everywhere. I turned my head and the many small rays of sunlight that pierced through the dense foliage lit up our paths. I would have enjoyed it more if I wasn't worrying about how we would get out of there and where exactly the dark stone was.

Suddenly Pearl stopped in front of a tree and looked up, meowing and pawing at the trunk. Detective Grey and I looked at each other, then walked up to the tree and looked up too.

"What is it?" Rachel said, panting at the end of her sentence after catching up to us as quickly as she could. "What are we looking at?"

She didn't get any answer, even though she was standing right behind us. There was a small, irritated huff and I heard her step forward, leaning her shoulder against mine as she too, looked up.

"Oh."

Above us, looking down at us with an equally curious face - albeit with some malice in it - was a monkey.

The fact that we'd seen a monkey in a forest wasn't the real issue, though. It was more concerning that this monkey wore a dirty, ratty shirt, with the sleeves cut off at the arms and unbuttoned, with most of the lower half of the shirt missing.

Then the monkey spoke to us, scratching its neck and giving us all a nasty look.

"Never seen a monkey before?"

"Err—"

He didn't let Rachel finish. "Are you coming up or not? I'm the only one here who knows where to go next."

We dropped our faces down to eye level and glanced at each other, our faces speaking for us. Rachel looked confused, probably wondering why we could hear the monkey too. Detective Grey looked irritated and resigned, as if he already knew what my answer would be, but didn't want to have to deal with the annoying monkey.

And me? I don't know what I looked like, but I knew what I felt—pure hope. I looked up at the monkey again. It looked bored, and was fiddling with a small hole in its shirt. When it ended up creating a bigger hole it grimaced and looked back at us, letting go of the shirt once it caught me looking.

"Well, are you coming? I don't have all day, you know."

*** ***

His name was Bobo, he told us later, after we'd managed to climb up into the branches of the tree and Pearl had nearly clawed his eyes out for laughing when I slipped and nearly fell out of the tree as I climbed up. The branches on this particular tree were thick and sturdy, and to my surprise I found myself getting very comfortable a few minutes after I first sat down.

We sat in a circle around Bobo, at his insistence: Rachel was on his left, and to my right, I sat across from him, and Detective Grey was on the other side. Pearl was curled up in my lap, enjoying being petted as I nervously scratched her ear, hoping for the best.

"What'dya got to eat?"

I sat and stared at Detective Grey. *What did we have to eat, and, did we have enough to share?*

Bobo refused to say anything until he got something to eat, so we sat in silence while I glanced at the others. *Monkeys don't eat cats right?...*

I had no idea what Detective Grey was thinking, but I wondered what we could give our host. I didn't have anything that I thought a monkey could reasonably eat – *were monkeys able to tolerate trail mix, even though they were omnivores?*

I pulled it out of my backpack anyway, lifting it up for him to see.

"Bobo?" I said hesitantly. "This is trail mix. It's a combination of dried—"

"No, no, he doesn't want that," Rachel said, waving her hand dismissively. She zipped her bag open and pulled out a bunch of bananas, handing them to the monkey.

"Monkeys prefer bananas, don't they?"

Bobo's lips stretched back into an approximation of a smile, only this was creepier and looked like he wanted to bite us. He reached out for the bananas, swinging his forearm to the right in a strange motion, and brought his forearm back to—

To smack the bunch of bananas out of Rachel's hands and onto the ground. We watched, stunned as the bananas flew in a large curve through the air and fell with a sad thump in the soil some distance from the tree. Then we looked back up at the monkey, whose face was now full of rage.

"I can't eat bananas! Don't you know that?"

I wanted to mention that there was no way we could have known that but decided it was better to let the monkey rant. I didn't want his anger turned towards me—*who knows if he would push me out of the tree or something?*

Bobo went on a whole rant about how some witch had cursed him with being unable to eat bananas for the rest of his life after he'd stolen and eaten all the bananas on her little plantation. I felt sorry for him, but most of my pity quickly died when the rant went on and on. Rachel looked more annoyed than I did, glancing mournfully at her bananas which had already shrunk in number since the bunch had been taken from by various animals over the course of Bobo's rant.

Finally, he ran out of steam and his face settled into a mask of calm.

"Give me this... trail meat," he said, after a long and uncomfortable silence in which he just stared at us, and we tried not to break his gaze.

"Trail mix," I corrected, using the gentlest tone I could but still afraid it would set him off. Fortunately for me it didn't, so despite the disgust I felt watching Bobo tear through the pack and stuff everything into his mouth, I watched patiently until he was ready to address us.

Finally, when he'd stuffed the rest of the food into his mouth, he wiped his mouth roughly and sneered at us.

"Not as good as bananas. What do you want to know?"

I opened my mouth and closed it again. I wasn't ready for the question. *What do I want to know?*

Detective Grey came to my rescue. "We'd like to know how to get out of here—we're looking for the Dark Stone, and if you have any information about the poison that killed our friend, we'd be very grateful."

Bobo snorted. "Hmm. The Dark Stone. Boring." His eyes lit up again. "That poison, however—describe it."

Detective Grey and I exchanged a look. I took the lead this time, explaining exactly what had happened when Diana took the poison-laced tea. Bobo nodded at my explanations, and when I was done he clapped his hands together in glee.

"This is more like it! Something that actually interests me. I know what it is—but I'm not telling you until you solve my test."

I straightened up in anticipation of the answer, but quickly deflated again when he mentioned a puzzle. Of course, it couldn't be that easy. Things never were around here.

I sighed. "What is your puzzle?"

He grinned at me, but I wasn't sure if it was supposed to reassure me or be malicious. It certainly looked like he was threatening me.

"Don't look so glum—I promise it's not that hard."

So you say.

"All you have to do is climb down, and go west for a bit until you reach a clearing with a large stone in the center. There's a puzzle carved into it. Solve it, and come back."

We looked at each other. *Was it really that easy?*

"I don't have all day, you know," Bobo said again, and we scurried out of the tree.

Finding the clearing wasn't hard, thanks to Detective Grey's handy compass. The puzzle was ridiculously easy too, and I felt a little cheated as we headed back to Bobo's tree. The monkey seemed smart, so why didn't he just solve it himself?

I wasn't going to look a gift horse in the mouth though, so I didn't ask any of the other questions running through my mind when we made it back to him. Instead, I repeated the questions we'd already asked.

He grew animated at the mention of the poison, but Rachel urged him to tell us about the Dark Stone first. He shot an irritated look at her but answered.

"You'll find it eventually. Just keep on going the way you've been going."

Rachel muttered that he wasn't very helpful and nearly fell out of the tree from the look he gave her. Then he turned to me.

"The poison you've told me about is a rare one, heh heh, never thought I'd actually hear about it. I'd thought it was a myth, but it is real," he said with some wonder.

I was growing impatient, but I reined in my irritation and asked politely, "Do you know what it's called?"

He snickered. "Do I? Of course I do! Who could forget something like that, with a weird name like that? It's called Xenovex. Strange name, that."

And with that, he jumped into the closest tree and left us to our own thoughts.

8

Lancelot

It was a relief to step out of the humid heat of the forest, but it was even more of a relief to be away from Bobo and his disdainful malice. He hadn't done anything to us, to be fair, but I couldn't help feeling that there was something darker lurking behind the monkey's face. *We probably won't have to do much to trigger whatever it was.*

Even Rachel heaved a sigh as we stepped into another strange place and the door vanished behind us.

I was just glad that encounter was over, and that we'd gotten something out of it. We were nowhere closer to the Dark Stone than we'd been after we'd stepped into the maze, but at least we knew what Diana had been poisoned with now.

Xenovex.

It didn't sound like something that had existed for centuries, more like a laboratory-manufactured compound. Maybe that was just the modern name, and the actual name had been lost in time. Who knew? Either way, it was a start.

I took in our new setting. We were in a corridor of stone this time, in what seemed to be an old castle. We had come out of a door in the wall, which had vanished into the stone after we were all through to the other side. Opposite the wall was a rectangular window, with no glass in it or curtains over it, and quickly we went to it and looked out.

There was a large yard, if I could call it that, below us, and high stone walls with towers on the left and right surrounded the yard. There was no exit or entrance in this yard, but I had a feeling if we went out and followed the walls to their natural meeting point we would find a gate, and quite possibly, a moat and a drawbridge. Beyond the walls it was all green – green fields, a green hill rising in the distance, a forest beyond the left tower. The sun shone down on the yard, and everything was still and quiet.

It was a nice type of quiet, which was soon broken by Rachel.

"Where *are* we?" she asked, childlike wonder in her tone, placing her hands on the edge of the window and leaning into the window, looking around with wide eyes. Detective Grey frowned at her and pulled her back by the arm.

"Careful," he muttered, distracted by the sight too. "You'll fall out."

Rachel scoffed, taking her arm out of his grasp gently. "I'll be fine." She didn't go back to leaning out of the window though, content to just look out. "Where are we anyway? What do you guys think?"

I shrugged, looking away from the window and at the corridor around us. The walls were bare except for the metal sconces hanging off the walls at intervals all throughout the corridor, as far as I could see. "If I had to guess," I said, turning back to her, "I'd say we were in the medieval era. Or a period when there were still castles. I'm not a history expert, so I can't really say…"

Just then, Diana's ghost floated out of the wall beside us and pointed down the corridor, where Pearl was looking.

She's come to help again?

We followed her finger with our gazes, but after a few moments of seeing and hearing nothing, I looked at her, confused. It was frustrating that I couldn't communicate with her—I was so sure there would be a lot she could tell me that would be helpful.

Since she couldn't say anything, we just stuck with the tried and tested method of communication for people who couldn't speak to each other: *asking her questions that she answered in charades.*

"Did you see someone coming?" I asked. Diana shook her head.

Detective Grey went next. "Is there someone around here we need to see?"

She nodded frantically. I was a little surprised, but when I thought about it, *how else would we get to where we wanted to go?* We'd already seen that this maze wasn't the regular maze, so it shouldn't have been surprising.

Detective Grey cocked his head back an inch as if he was surprised at the answer too. Then he nodded and asked another question.

"Is this person the only one in this place?"

Diana nodded, and we all relaxed. Speaking to one person who was probably going to test us was already nerve-wracking. We didn't need the additional challenge of dealing with other people who might not be helpful and might try to hinder us.

"Is the person in that direction?" Rachel asked, pointing in the direction Diana had shown us only a few minutes before. Diana nodded. We glanced at each other.

"I guess we know what to do next," Rachel said, pushing off the wall she'd been leaning against. In sync we all turned and walked down the corridor, Pearl coming to walk next to my feet as Diana floated ahead of us.

"I wonder what the test will be this time," Rachel spoke up again just as we got to the end of the corridor. It turned sharply to the right, where a large wooden door stood in a short recess. Diana floated through the door seconds before Detective Grey moved forward to open the door.

"Diana? Where are you going?" I called out. I felt silly after doing it, but I couldn't help worrying. She might have been incorporeal at the moment, but it didn't mean she couldn't be hurt.

She poked her head out of the door and nodded at me, then disappeared again as Detective Grey opened the door. There she was, on the other side, waiting for us. I looked away from the mirth on her face and inspected our new environment. We were stepping into a large room that spanned almost the distance we'd walked to get here, both in how wide and how long it was.

I didn't get the chance to fully admire the deep red tapestries that decorated all four walls though, because in the center of the room stood a man in a suit of armor.

His sword was in his hands, the tip of it pushed into the stone floor. He looked very much like he was wearing an actual suit of armor, and the only reason we could tell there was someone behind all that metal was because his visor was up and we could see his steely gray eyes glaring at us.

"You three are dressed strangely," he said, and somehow I could understand him, even though he was most definitely not speaking modern English. "Especially the women. Are you from the Order of Oscuros?"

Rachel shook her head frantically, and Detective Grey frowned. I hesitated, however—the word *Oscuros* sounded familiar for some reason as if I'd heard it before, and his sharp eyes caught the brief moment of hesitation.

"You are one of them?" he asked, his eyes getting darker as he lifted his sword and pointed it at me. Detective Grey pulled me to the side, out of the line of fire, but the sword just pivoted to face me.

"Speak!"

I shook my head just like Rachel had done, but there was fear behind my actions.

"I don't know who this 'Order of Oscuros' is! I swear—it just sounded familiar to me like I've heard it before."

He left his sword pointed at me for a few more seconds, and I was starting to think about running before he dropped it again. I breathed a huge sigh of relief, but he wasn't done with us.

"If you are not with them, then why are you here?" he demanded.

Detective Grey stepped forward. "We're looking for the Dark Stone. The maze led us here."

The knight's grip tightened around the handle of his sword, and he stared off into the distance.

"The Dark Stone. Yes, I remember something of that nature. But why should I help you?"

He stared at us with his piercing gaze, as if daring one of us to say something. Rachel took the challenge, stepping forward and nodding at him.

"A knight such as yourself follows the rules of chivalry closely. Isn't one of the rules to help whoever's in need?" she asked.

He snorted.

"The code of chivalry does not use those words, but the intent is the same. Fine, I will listen to your story and then judge for myself if you are worthy of my knowledge. What are your names, and where are you from?"

We each gave him a brief history of our lives over the next twenty or thirty minutes, and I learned things about my companions that I couldn't have imagined. For instance, that Detective Grey used to be quite the troublemaker in school, or that the first animal Rachel spoke to was a snail in her mother's garden.

"That is quite enough of that," the knight said at last, holding up a gauntleted hand. "Now I will tell you about myself. I am Sir Lancelot, and I am very much pleased to make your acquaintance."

Rachel gasped, her eyes growing wide and she covered her mouth with her hands.

"Are you *the* Sir Lancelot? One of the Knights of the Round Table—?"

Lancelot's face darkened, and Rachel snapped her mouth shut, aware she'd somehow said the wrong thing. I noticed how tightly he was gripping his sword, and I quickly tried to do some damage control before he decided he wanted to strike us down for the insult to his person.

"I'm sure Rachel didn't mean it that way—"

He scoffed. "Of course she didn't mean it that way. Nobody remembers *me* and the sacrifices I made, dealing with those knavish curs from the damned Order of Oscuros, but the first thing that springs to their minds when they hear the name Lancelot is that damned myth—"

Rachel gasped at his words, but I cut in before she could say something like "Lancelot's not real?" and anger him again.

"What did the Order of Oscuros do?" I asked.

He eyed me, irritated for whatever reason, but he still answered.

"What didn't they do? They stole, murdered, sacrificed people to their Dark Lord, and more. One of my trusted friends was one of them in disguise, and when I refused to join his pathetic cult he stabbed me in the back and left me to die."

I didn't know what to say to that, but luckily Sir Lancelot loved to hear the sound of his own voice.

"That is all in the past now, and it cannot be changed. Come, duel me, so I can test your worthiness and hence be rid of you."

Detective Grey stepped forward before I could even ask what exactly Sir Lancelot meant, and the other man gave him a nod. He stepped back and took a sword off the armor rack behind him, which I hadn't noticed all the time I'd been in the room.

"Do you know what you're doing?" I hissed at Detective Grey, who just shrugged my concern off.

"Don't worry, Charlotte. I know what I'm doing."

I wasn't convinced, but I doubted I was going to change his mind. So I let him do what he wanted and retreated to the side of the room with Rachel, hoping that Detective Grey didn't do something stupid like get himself killed.

The duel, if you could call it that, was nerve-wracking. Every time Sir Lancelot and Detective Grey crossed swords all I could imagine was the sword slipping past Detective Grey's defenses and burying itself between his ribs. Rachel didn't feel the same way, clapping wildly and whooping whenever Detective Grey got the upper hand.

To my surprise, Detective Grey threw the sword in the crack of the charging shoulder armor in front of him. Sir Lancelot groaned and let down his sword. Rachel whispered to me that Detective Grey had just won, though it was by a slight margin.

All I cared about was that he was unharmed and that we could finally get the information we needed from Sir Lancelot, who looked sulky at being beaten.

He told us about the Dark Stone, and added a little more to my surprise and delight. He confirmed that the Dark Stone could indeed resurrect a dead person, and then more. He didn't tell us what *more* was, because just then a door appeared in the wall of the room, and we didn't even wait for him to say anything before making our way to it.

I had a best friend to resurrect, and I wasn't spending any more time with this bitter knight.

9

To the Future

We left Lancelot's castle as fast as we could before he could challenge us to another duel. The man was bitter and more than a little angry—not a great combination if we were searching for someone to actually help us.

The door slammed shut behind us, most likely courtesy of Sir Lancelot, and after looking over my shoulder to make sure the knight was truly gone, I sighed in relief and turned back to the strange sight in front of me. My companions were already staring at it, and even Diana's ghostly mouth hung slightly open as she took in our new environment.

I couldn't help staring as well. Everyone except for Pearl, who looked as unbothered as ever, was in awe of the futuristic setting that we found ourselves in. The place was cyberpunk from the neon lights to the dark skies and bustling nightlife.

Well, the "bustling nightlife" wasn't really telling of a cyberpunk-ish setting. We could find that anywhere, but what was truly telling was the number of people who walked past our alley with metal arms, legs, eye/eyes, and there was even one woman whose entire body *(minus her head?)* was made completely out of metal.

Detective Grey was the first one to recover the use of his tongue.

"There are a lot of people around—"

"We can all see that, Detective Grey," Rachel said.

He gave her an annoyed look.

"I know. I was about to say that we're going to stick out like a sore thumb if we leave this alley, but we can't stay here forever. Even worse, we don't know exactly where we're supposed to go or what we're supposed to do. It's possible that this part of the maze won't be the same as the ones we've seen before."

"Oh." Her mouth closed with an audible snap, and she turned away from him to inspect the rest of the alley. I left her and Detective Grey, who had gone a step further and was poking at the walls, to their work while I kept on looking out of the alley. Something drew my attention to the people, but even after minutes of staring hard at each one that walked past the alley I still hadn't found anything that scratched my itch of curiosity.

Behind me, Rachel and Detective Grey didn't seem to be having much luck either. Rachel stepped back from eyeballing the graffiti-covered wall and huffed.

"If there's a secret entrance or something, I haven't found it."

Detective Grey straightened up, turned to us, and shook his head.

"Nothing here. All I've found out was that graffiti still exists here, for some reason."

I pursed my lips impatiently at him, understanding Rachel's mood moments earlier.

"I could have told you that if you'd asked. I'm sure even in the early centuries people were drawing on structures they weren't supposed to."

He gave me a small grin and considered the entrance of the alley again, watching the people going by. Strangely, none of them ever looked into the alley, and it made me feel like I was invisible, which I was happy to be.

"Does anything seem strange to you about these people?" he asked, moments later.

I nodded. When I realized he wasn't looking at me, I answered.

"Yeah, but I can't say exactly what it is."

Rachel poked her head in the space between us and looked at the entrance of the alley.

"They act like this place doesn't exist," she said after a moment, referring to the alley we were still loitering in.

I turned to her, surprised. "I thought that too, but how is it important?"

She shook her head and stepped back. "I'm not sure. Usually, most people would at least glance at the alley, even if they had no intention of stepping into it. Also, lots of people with electronic eyes have walked past us. Again, I'm not sure, but from the video games I've played, don't those eyes take in more information than the normal human eye? Can't they see our heat signatures or something?"

Detective Grey stared at her for a moment and stepped forward.

"There's only one way to find out," he said. I grabbed his arm before he could take another step.

"What are you doing?" I gasped.

He patted my hand and gently loosened my grip on his arm, taking my fingers off his arm one by one.

"Charlotte, it'll be okay. I just need to test something."

I grabbed his sleeve this time. "And you're sure it won't put us in trouble? This looks like something we can't handle if everything goes south."

He frowned for a second as if he was in thought, but then the confidence came back to his face the next moment.

"I'm ninety-nine percent sure," he said.

I frowned, not liking even those odds, but I let him go.

"If you're sure," I repeated, a hint of warning in my tone. He just nodded at me and went on. I looked down at Pearl who was playing with a small metal object that had wires sticking out of it. *She doesn't seem alarmed, so everything is fine, right?*

"You can't rely on Pearl all the time," Rachel spoke up from behind me. I looked at her, startled. She'd voiced exactly what I was thinking.

I reluctantly nodded. "I feel like I'm getting complacent. Pearl obviously has been a great help, but she hasn't always had the answers to some problems. I have to remember that."

I turned back to Detective Grey, feeling strangely vulnerable after sharing all that with Rachel. It was the kind of thing I would say to Diana, and I swallowed the heat that had balled up in my throat. There was no time for that now—I had to focus.

Ahead of us, blocking out most of the hazy pink and blue light that streamed into the alleyway from a signboard high above and opposite the alley, stood Detective Grey. He lifted his arm and reached out like he was expecting some resistance. When there was none, he stepped forward.

I held my breath, but nothing happened. He was just a man standing in front of an alley while the rest of the world moved on and around him. The strangest thing was, that none of the people even looked at him or gave him an annoyed look for taking up space. Every single one of them walked past him.

Detective Grey stepped back into the alley, grinning at us.

"Told you nothing would happen," he said.

Rachel ran up to him. "What did you do?" she demanded.

Just as he was about to answer her, I gasped and pointed behind them. "Guys! Behind you!"

Detective Grey's eyes narrowed, and he pulled Rachel with him as he ran back to Pearl and me with amazingly quick reflexes. Rachel sputtered indignantly, but she grew quiet when he finally let her go and she was able to see what I'd been staring at.

Behind them, a lanky robot with shaky limbs that looked like they'd been hastily put together and a head much too big for its body stepped into the alley, the square holes I'd call its eyes blinking blue and black at us.

"I thought you said nothing would happen," Rachel whispered furiously to Detective Grey, who waved an arm at her and hissed that now wasn't the time. I kept my eyes on the robot who took two shaky steps towards us and stopped. I was so tense I couldn't even turn back to see what Pearl thought of the new situation, even though I desperately wanted to. It didn't matter that I'd promised myself not to rely on her so much.

The robot swayed in place, and I was torn between a probably irrational fear for my life and worry that the robot would suddenly collapse.

"Greetings," the robot said. Its computer-generated voice emanated from a square of punctured holes in the lower part of its face, looking very much like a speaker.

"Uh, hi?" I said, leaning over to Rachel and whispering, "Aren't you the animal whisperer? Do something!"

She gave me a nasty look. "That's not an animal, Charlotte."

"Indeed, I am not," the robot said again in its staccato voice. "I am M2-dash-S2. The dash does not need speaking. It is written that way."

"Okay?" I replied, unsure why we needed to know that. "I'm Charlotte, and these are my friends..."

The robot stayed quiet long enough for me to make the introductions, as weird as it made me feel, but immediately after I was done speaking it spoke again.

"That is good to know. There is no time to waste. Find the code. It is here. I will tell you what it means."

M2-S2's eyes turned black, and the alley grew quiet again. I realized then that there'd been a low humming in the background, but we hadn't noticed it until M2-S2 had gone to sleep, or whatever it was doing.

We turned to each other. "What now?" Rachel asked.

Detective Grey had already sprung into action, inspecting the walls again. "Find the code, like it said. It's probably in the graffiti."

Somehow, neither Rachel nor I had any questions. Instead, we went to work, turning our flashlights on the wall and reading the graffiti with such intensity anyone who saw us would think we were studying for a test.

"There's nothing here," Rachel said, straightening up five minutes later and wincing. I winced too. I'd been crouching for too long, reading the graffiti at the bottom of the wall and my joints were protesting.

"You too, Charlotte?" he asked, not looking at us.

"Nothing," I confirmed.

He hummed and turned around. "I think I found something."

Rachel and I crowded around him, and then we saw it. Where the light of his flashlight hit the walls, letters had been burnt into the wall somehow by a concentrated point of heat. I had no idea how it was done, or how we missed it before, but I was happy we'd finally found something.

Rachel read it out. "LD... 240... A120... E30L07."

Just as the last digit left her mouth, M2-S2 whirred back to life.

"Well done. You have found the code. You can now access the message in the code."

The robot went quiet again. Rachel looked at us, puzzled.

"I thought it was supposed to tell us the message."

I stepped forward, keeping my eyes on it. I wasn't completely sure of what I was about to do, but it was worth a shot. And if I was right—

"M2-S2, what is the message in the code?" I asked.

The robot's eyes turned blue again. "Follow the trail to the Dark Stone. Beware of the Order of Oscuros, descendant of Appleman."

My eyes widened. Appleman—my grandmother's maiden name had been Appleman! How did it know that?

"M2-S2, what do you know about Elena Appleman?"

The robot whirred noisily for a moment, then spoke again.

"Elena Appleman. Witch. Christened by the Order of Oscuros. Gained her powers from the Order of Oscuros."

I wanted to ask more questions, like how exactly it knew these things, and how all of this worked. Rachel pulled me away and toward the wall where the code had appeared, where the new door now stood.

"Wait—" I tried to say, but she cut me short.

"Can Diana's body wait?" she asked, stepping through the door into a somewhat modern house. I turned back to look at the robot, sighing in disappointment when I discovered it was gone.

I'll find out later, I promised myself. I had so many questions, but for now, I had to resurrect Diana. I stepped through the door, and I felt the walls becoming solid behind me.

10

Casper

The next location shouldn't have surprised me after all I'd seen and experienced so far, but somehow it still did. The main reason for this was the atmosphere of the place—simply put, it was a haunted mansion.

How did I know it was haunted? Well, after we'd spent only one minute in the place, wandering from abandoned room to abandoned room and calling out for whoever owned the place or lived there to show themselves, a ghost popped out in my vision and screamed at us, laughing hysterically.

I was ashamed of how shrill my responding scream was, but I couldn't help myself. Rachel nearly fell over laughing at me, and Detective Grey wasn't any better. At least he had the decency to turn away from me, curling over Pearl in his arms like he was whispering to her, even though I could still see his shoulders shaking.

"Yeah, yeah, laugh it up," I grumbled, eyeing them with annoyance. In front of us the ghost cackled one last time and floated away.

Rachel finally stopped laughing and turned to me, wiping her eyes. "You have to admit that it was funny though."

I sniffed, pointing my nose in the air and walking ahead of them. "It wasn't, no matter what you say."

I heard their footsteps following after mine, and I carried on pushing open every door we came across. The majority of them were unlocked, and all the rooms we looked into had furniture covered in a thick layer of dust that turned everything a light brown.

The ghosts kept popping in and out, from the walls, the floor, and appearing out of nowhere in my face sometimes, but I'd learned my lesson. They still gave me a shock whenever they popped up, but now I could control my reactions.

We seemed to be on one of the upper floors of the mansion, as we'd seen when we looked out, and finally we came to the landing and the staircase. I looked at my companions.

"Should we go down or carry on checking each door?" I asked. The corridor still went on beyond the landing, and I wondered exactly how large this house was.

Rachel shrugged. "I say let's go down," she replied. "I feel like we're not really going to find anything different from what we've seen so far."

I turned to Detective Grey. "And you?"

He shrugged too. "Let's go down."

So we did. It turned out that there were only two upper floors, and we got to the ground floor quickly, making the decision not to stop at the first floor since it looked very much like the second floor.

The ground floor was different in the variety of its rooms. The foyer that the stairs led us into was completely bare of any furniture, but the four doors that led out of it were more interesting. The first one on the right led out of the house, but the house was surrounded by a thick hedge of thorny thickets that killed any hope of us getting out that way.

The next two doors led to the kitchen and out into the garden, but on trying the last door we finally had some luck. It led into a small corridor, and after that was clearly a living room. There was no time to admire the living room, which was well-kept and clean, in stark contrast to the rest of the house, because we'd finally found someone other than ourselves who wasn't a ghost.

The pale dark-haired man sat in an armchair facing the door we'd just come through, and though he was quite handsome there was something about him that unsettled me.

"Welcome," he said, giving us a smile too full of teeth for my taste. And were those fangs in his mouth?

"Are you..." Rachel trailed off, and he helped her finish the statement, a smile on his lips all the while.

"A vampire? Why, yes I am. You've never seen one before?"

She shook her head and turned to me. I raised an eyebrow at her.

"Why would you assume *I* have seen one before?"

She shrugged. "Well, you're always getting into weird stuff. I mean, your cat can do strange things. Why is it so far-fetched to assume you've met a vampire before?

"Well, I haven't. Are you going to do anything to us?" I asked. Immediately after I said it, I cringed at how rude it sounded.

"Sorry about that. It was rude—"

He held up his hand, and I stopped talking. "It's fine. I probably would have taken offense if it was anyone else, but Tiana's daughter gets a pass from me anytime."

My head snapped back at that.

"My mother? You knew my mother?"

He nodded, looking a little confused, and dropped the book he'd been reading before we walked in onto his lap. He unbuttoned his sleeve, rolling up the sleeve to expose a bandage over most of his forearm.

"I know her," he corrected. "She saved my life—she's still saving it, in fact."

I shook my head and stepped forward.

"I thought vampires were immortal," I said. I had no idea why I said that, when what I truly wanted to say was *how do you know my mother?*

Rachel shared the same sentiment, because under her breath but still audible enough for me to hear her, she muttered, "*That's* what you're asking?"

The only person who didn't look surprised was the vampire in question. Even Detective Grey gave me a look while Pearl meowed in his lap.

The vampire shook his head. "We are, but we can still be injured, and this was a particularly nasty injury that I can't heal myself. That's where your mother comes in."

He shook his head again and sat up straighter. "Where are my manners? I haven't introduced myself—I'm Casper. Sit down, please. And who are you?"

We told him our names, although it was obvious he was only really interested in me. I was the last one to speak, and he leaned slightly toward me as I spoke.

"Well, I'm Charlotte, Tiana's daughter." Even saying her name made me angry. I had somehow clenched my fists, and I let my fists relax slowly. I saw Casper's eyes go to my fists, but he didn't say anything about it. Instead he smiled at me.

"It's nice to finally meet you. Tiana speaks highly of you."

That raised my eyebrows.

"Really?" I said, failing to keep the skepticism out of my tone. Casper leaned back in his chair, steepled his fingers in front of me with his gaze firmly fixed on mine all the while.

"You two are not on good terms? That was not the impression I got from her."

I shook my head. "I don't want to talk about it. Where are we, anyway?" I said, awkwardly changing the subject.

Fortunately for me he accepted the subject change gracefully and went with the flow.

"It's one of my hideouts. There are a few individuals who would like to see me dead, for one reason or another, and I have to stay here until I've regained my strength."

"You couldn't have chosen a less creepy place?" Rachel muttered, eyeing a ghost that floated down from the ceiling, upside down, and was now hovering in front of her face.

Casper shrugged, making the motion feel even more elegant than it could ever have done on someone else.

"This one is quiet. And the ghosts don't bother me."

"Do you know about the Dark Stone?" Detective Grey asked. "We need to find it as soon as possible."

Casper surveyed him. "I do, but before I tell you, what do you need it for?"

Detective Grey looked at me. I spoke, "Someone promised my friend's resurrection if we brought back the Dark Stone and gave it to them. I have no idea who that was, but I can only hope they were telling the truth."

He looked confused. "Why didn't you ask your mother? She might not have been able to revive your friend, but she could have helped before she died."

I swallowed my rising anger at the insinuation that I could have done more to save Diana, and when I replied my voice was cold.

"Diana was poisoned. She took one sip of poisoned tea and died minutes later. I'm not sure there's anything anyone could have done."

Casper shook his head. "I'm sorry to hear that, and I'm also sorry for bringing up any bad blood between you and your mother. I can't help thinking that she could have helped with your search for the Dark Stone though—what was the poison that killed your friend?"

"Xenovex," we all said in unison. For some reason Casper's eyebrows went up.

"Xenovex? Well, this gets more and more complex."

I was at the edge of my seat. "Why do you say that? Do you know anything about Xenovex? Any little bit of information you can offer would be so helpful."

The mood in the room had changed. We had been sort of down, drained by all we'd gone through so far, and finding out that there was a possible answer to our questions revitalized us.

Casper looked slightly embarrassed. "I only know what I know because of Tiana. As it turns out, she has the last of the Xenovex in the world with her. It's not a good look for her now, given what you've told me, I know. It's also possible that someone stole the poison from your mother."

I sank into my seat, leaning back to let his words sit in my mind. I didn't have the best relationship with my mother, which was an understatement, but I had no idea why she would kill Diana, if she was the killer. I was fairly sure she didn't even know who Diana was.

"This doesn't mean anything, Charlotte," Detective Grey said, reaching across to pat my shoulder. It comforted me a little, and I nodded at him.

"I know," I said, and turned back to Casper. "Now what can you tell us about the Dark Stone?"

11

PICKLESQUARE

We left Casper quickly after he finally gave us a lead to the Dark Stone. Detective Grey kept trying to give me meaningful looks, but I pretended I was laser-focused on the Dark Stone and the fact that we were almost close to it. I knew what he wanted. He wanted me to talk about it, *it* being the whole situation with my mother who had suddenly reappeared in my life.

I didn't want to talk about it though, so I left that topic squarely alone. He must have understood what I wanted, because he didn't say anything about it anymore. Casper had said we didn't even need his help to locate the Dark Stone. According to him, if we'd kept going we would have found it soon. It was gratifying to know that we were that close to our goal and hopefully to reviving Diana, but I could have done without the reminder that my mother existed.

We were back in the maze proper, walking through the darkened corridors again. Somehow no one wanted to start up a conversation, not even Rachel, who had been so bubbly at the beginning. Diana's ghost floated a bit ahead of us, a sober reminder of the reason I was even down there at all. Detective Grey and I walked beside each other in silent but comfortable companionship, and I was starting to feel a little better as we went on.

Maybe I was overreacting. Just because Casper, a vampire I'd just met, knew my mother, it didn't mean I would have to see her too. There was no need to bring down everyone's mood just because I didn't feel so good about something that might never even happen.

On the other hand, what if she was involved in Diana's death? That was another thing that tugged at my thoughts, and my frown only grew deeper thinking about it. Casper seemed hesitant to tell me anything about why my not-so-regular mother would know anything about a mysterious centuries-old poison, but he trusted her. Did that count for something?

I shook my head, as if to clear it of the thoughts that wouldn't let me be, and took in a deep breath, letting it out maybe a bit too loudly. Rachel looked over her shoulder at me with a raised eyebrow, and I shook my head again. She didn't look reassured like I intended, but she just nodded and turned back around.

Detective Grey nudged my arm with his elbow. "Are you okay?" he leaned over and whispered. I looked up at him, forced a small smile and nodded.

"I'm fine," I said, but even I didn't believe it. Neither did he, but like before, he took my response at face value and left me alone. I was grateful for it.

We walked on a bit more, not one door in sight. At first it wasn't a concern. I assumed that since we'd gone through so many doors at once maybe it would take some time for the next one to appear. I figured everybody else had the same thought, so we went on in silence.

Eventually Rachel stopped in the middle of the corridor, running her flashlight over the walls on both sides of her. I looked at the walls too, carefully, in case I missed anything that might point to a secret entrance or passage. I found nothing.

"Why are we stopping?" Detective Grey asked. Diana had floated back to us to hover near the walls too, curiosity on her face.

I looked at Rachel, who just switched off her flashlight and put her hands on her hips, turning to face us.

"I don't know about you, but I'm getting tired of just walking with nothing important in sight. Just walls, walls, and oh look! More walls!"

I furrowed my eyebrows, wondering why she was suddenly taking issue with the fact that we'd been down here for so long. She never had any problem with it earlier, so why was it suddenly an issue?

"I don't know what to say to you, Rachel, but I'm sure we'll soon get to another door," I said at last, nothing else coming to mind. I could have probably framed it in a better way, because her face crumpled and she got even more annoyed when she heard what I had to say.

I exhaled slowly. I didn't care too much about Rachel's comfort for several reasons. First was that she was the one who'd invited herself on the journey with us, and therefore she had no right to complain. Second, she could always leave if she wanted, but I doubted bringing up the idea of walking through the dark, musty corridors of the maze alone would make her happier. If anything, she would be even more annoyed with me.

I looked at Detective Grey, hoping he would be able to help. His face was blank in that way it got when he had mentally distanced himself from a situation, and I knew he wasn't going to be much help.

I sighed inwardly and turned back to Rachel. I was about to open my mouth and offer her whatever comfort I could scrounge up, but then she heaved a large sigh and turned around, switching on her flashlight again.

"Never mind," she said. "Let's just go."

Detective Grey and I shared another glance as she began to walk away, Diana looking between her departing form and us before floating after her. I knew he had the same question I did: *why did she change her mind all of a sudden?* I wasn't going to take her sudden revitalization for granted, so I decided to keep an eagle eye out on Rachel and followed them.

Detective Grey's footsteps echoed after mine in the next moment. We walked on, and just as Rachel said, all we saw were walls, walls, and even more walls. I was starting to get tired of walking and was just about to request that we all stop for a break.

Then I caught my foot on something sticking up out of the ground, and I almost fell flat on my face, if not for Detective Grey's strong grip holding me up before my face kissed the ground. I thanked him as I straightened up, my heart still racing from the near-miss, then I turned my flashlight towards the ground to take a look at what I'd stumbled over.

"Uh... guys? I think you should see this," I said, staring at the lever poking out of the ground.

Detective Grey, only two steps away, came back immediately. Rachel, however, stopped in the middle of the path some distance ahead of us, huffing loudly.

"What is it now?" she said, irritation coloring her tone. When no one answered her, she huffed loudly again and stomped back to us.

"Well? What do I have to see that you couldn't just tell me about it—oh. Is that a lever?"

I nodded and looked up at my companions. "What do you guys think? Should we pull it?"

I wasn't prepared for Rachel to crouch down and pull it, muttering about how we were wasting so much time. We held our breaths for a second, then when nothing happened, let them go.

"Really? I was expecting something more—"

We never got to find out what Rachel was expecting, because just then the familiar grinding sounded and she got to her feet quickly, stepping back with the rest of us as the grinding rang out around us. Nothing changed in our surroundings though, and we sighed simultaneously.

"So much for that," I said, shooting the lever a disappointed look. "Sorry about that guys, I really thought it would lead us somewhere."

Rachel brushed dust off her knees. She didn't seem as annoyed as she'd been a few moments earlier.

"Eh, it's fine. Let's keep going."

I exchanged a look with Detective Grey as she went back to her position at the head of our little party. She'd switched up so fast—was it just false cheer or was she just the type that forgave very easily? Detective Grey smiled at me encouragingly, and we continued on our way, walking faster to catch up with Rachel.

Whatever it was, I didn't care much. I preferred a jovial but annoying Rachel to an annoyed one that kept being saucy. We had barely walked for more than five minutes before Rachel let out a squeal.

We raced up to her.

"Rachel!" I called as I ran. "What is it—?"

I skidded to a stop and stared like Rachel was doing. It seemed that out of nowhere an entrance to another room had appeared in the middle of the corridor. The rectangular entrance led into a dark room, lit up here and there by the beams from our flashlights. Looking into the room, I couldn't see much, but it was clear that it was a fairly large room, and there was a breeze coming from somewhere high in the room.

"It wasn't here when I pointed my flashlight down the corridor before," Rachel said in excitement. I gave her a skeptical look.

"Are you sure?"

She rolled her eyes at me. "Yes, Charlotte. I have 20/20 vision—and this definitely wasn't here before."

"Not even a door?" I asked, still unable to believe that a door had just materialized out of the blue.

She sighed and lifted her eyes to the ceiling. "Yes, Charlotte, it wasn't there before..."

"What is it?" I asked, wondering why she'd stopped speaking. She simply lifted a finger and pointed at the ceiling. I looked up too, and though I couldn't make much sense out of the complicated arrangement of pulleys, ropes, and a large block of wood, I could make an inference.

"That's the door?"

"It seems like the lever Rachel pulled back there was the mechanism to open this door," Detective Grey said from behind us.

"And what would have happened if we didn't see the lever or pull it?" I wondered. I wasn't expecting an answer, but Rachel answered anyway.

"I'm guessing we would have kept walking. Maybe we might have gotten lost in this place. Imagine if we never found our way out."

I suppressed a shudder at the image that came into my mind. "Let's just move on," I said.

"Yes, let's," Rachel agreed, and we stepped into the new room.

It was bare and dusty. The only area of interest in the entire room was the marble plinth that sat in the center of the room, and the marble rectangle on the floor. They were both made of the same material, but unlike the plinth, we couldn't open it. There were grooves around the marble rectangle where it had been placed into the stone around it, but it was hair thin and none of us could get our nails under it.

The plinth, however, had a square etched into its top. It was as thin as the rectangle below, but pushing down on one side of the square pushed the other side up, so we could get it out. As we finally lifted up the square to reveal a deep black sphere, Rachel pointed behind us.

"What's that?" she asked. We dropped the sphere back in its box and turned to look.

Another door, just like all the ones we'd gone through before, had appeared on the wall. The only difference this time was that it looked extremely familiar to me.

"Hey," I said. "That looks like my kitchen door."

Detective Grey went up to it and peered at it. Then he ran his hands over the door and stepped back.

"Charlotte, I think it is your kitchen door."

"Oh," was all I could think to say.

"What's it doing here?" Rachel asked.

I shrugged. How would I know? I looked at Detective Grey.

"We're going, right?"

He nodded. "Of course." He turned to Rachel and Diana. "I think you two should stay here and make sure no one else gets the Dark Stone—"

"Wait. That's the Dark Stone?" I cut in. It seemed so ordinary.

He nodded. "It's very possible that we've finally found it. Like I was saying, Rachel and Diana will stay here, while Charlotte and I will go through the door. Hopefully, we won't take too long. Does anyone have any questions or objections?"

We shook our heads. I waved goodbye to Diana before following Detective Grey through the door.

We came face to face with someone I thought I'd never set eyes on ever again. And it was done.

12

TIANA

"What are you doing here?"

I really need to stop being so shocked that no one wants to see us.

Things like this always happened to me. I'd encounter a reminder of someone or something, and in a few hours or a day I'd come in contact with said thing or person. I should have known when Casper brought up my mother that I'd eventually meet her—actually, I did know, somewhere deep down. I just hadn't wanted to think about it, and here I was, facing down my absent mother.

To her credit, she didn't look insulted by my accusing tone. If anything, she looked a bit contrite. The sight of the remorse on her face made me even more annoyed though. Who did she think she was, to waltz into my life after years without a word from her, and think that all it would take to make things better was an apology?

"Charlotte, I know—"

"You know what?" I cut in, already done with her presence in my house. "I don't want to hear whatever you have to say. It's five years too late, so thanks for coming, I guess, but you can leave now."

I folded my arms and turned away, facing the wall behind the couch I stood in front of and blinking the hot tears out of my eyes. Why was I crying? It irritated me even more, and I blinked rapidly until I'd managed to get rid of the tears that had built up in my eyes. The method didn't always work, but the universe must have been smiling down on me, because in a few moments my eyes were somewhat dry again.

I didn't hear any footsteps or anything that would indicate that my mother was leaving, so I turned around again and eyed her with annoyance.

"Is there a reason you're still here?" I asked. She opened her mouth to respond, but it was Detective Grey who stepped in and spoke to me.

"I know you're angry, Charlotte, but I think we need to sit and listen to what Tiana has to say. It might be important."

I raised my eyebrows at him. He was supposed to be on my side, but I pushed that thought away a moment later. It was too childish, and as much as I wanted to resent him for asking me to do the exact opposite of what I wanted to do at the present moment, I recognized that he was right. My mother, as flighty as she was, wouldn't be in my house without a concrete reason.

After all, if all she wanted to do was apologize to me, she could have just called or texted me, and I would have been fine with that. There was no reason to come all the way down to Picklesquare.

Unless she was being sincere, a voice in my head reminded me... a voice that sounded suspiciously like my grandmother's. I swatted the thought away mentally. I preferred to think that she was here for something more important than apologizing to the daughter she'd been cold to for years.

"Fine," I said finally, and they both relaxed subtly. I took two steps backward and plopped myself on the couch behind me, watching as Detective Grey and my mother did the same.

When everyone was settled, I asked again, "Why are you here, Tiana?" She winced at the use of her name, but I wasn't going to let her think we were still fine by calling her "Mom."

"Charlotte, I—"

I held up a hand to stop her, and when she paused, looking confused, I shook my head at her.

"I don't want your cheap apologies or anything. I just want to know why you're here, and it had better be for a good reason. Also, what is Xenovex, and how did it turn up in a teacup at Helena Parkson's tea party?"

She sighed and leaned back in her chair. It suddenly struck me how much older she looked. There were more lines on her face than I remembered, and more gray hairs than she'd had previously. It made me a little sad to think that she was growing old, and that in decades I'd probably be burying her, but I quickly buried that under my anger. Don't go soft, Charlotte.

"Well?" I prompted her after moments of waiting for an answer that wasn't coming anytime soon. She shot me a look that would have made me quake when I was fourteen, but all it did now was make me settle down just a bit.

"I'm getting to it, Charlie."

"Don't call me that." I couldn't stop myself from correcting her. She fixed eyes on me and took a sip from the tea cup she cradled in her hand.

"Charlotte, then. As I was about to say, I'm sorry about Diana, but I don't know what happened that day, or why it would end up at Helena Parkson's party, of all people," she said, muttering the last bit under her breath.

"What do you mean you don't know why? Casper said the last of the Xenovex was in your possession."

She shook her head. "Maybe it's not where I left it anymore. Charlotte, I don't carry it around. I never thought that it would go missing or someone would steal it. It was so obscure and only a few people besides myself and Casper knew I had it."

I wanted to let out another barb and say that maybe if she'd been more careful Diana would still be alive, but it would be dumb to keep on antagonizing the person who might have answers to some of my questions. I was still irritated at her for just popping up out of the blue and expecting that we would go back to the way we'd been before she'd left me to my grandmother, but I was also tired of everything—of being angry, of the hoops I'd had to jump through just to find the Dark Stone, of the sadness that still simmered in my gut and the gaping hole in my chest that hurt whenever I thought about Diana.

So I let the rage flow out of me with one exhale, and then, calmer than I thought I could be, asked, "And you have no idea who would want to steal it? Or why they would be interested in Diana?"

She shook her head. "I'm sorry, Charlotte. It's obvious how much she meant to you. I promise I'll do everything I can to help with whatever you're doing."

I shook my head. The offer was nice of her, but I didn't want to be around her more than I had to.

Detective Grey finally spoke up.

"You still haven't told us why you're in Picklesquare," he said.

She took another sip from her cup and placed it, saucer and all, on the small square table beside her armchair.

"I was getting to that, but yes, I'm not just here to see you, Charlotte."

Oh really? I couldn't tell.

The look on my face must have said what I was thinking, because after meeting my gaze she looked away, choosing to focus on Detective Grey instead.

"I'm in Picklesquare because I needed to speak with you, Charlotte. Two days ago, Elena Appleman was in my dreams, and then I saw her in real life. She said you're in danger." She turned to me, looking concerned. "And that you might need my help. So," she smiled at me awkwardly, "here I am."

I really didn't want to accept any help from her, but the thought of Diana and Detective Grey's raised eyebrow at me said rejecting the offer of help would be the most foolish thing I'd ever done in my life. Also, my mother seemed to know more about the supernatural than I did. It would irritate me endlessly when I eventually ended up asking for her help at some point, but it was unavoidable.

I sighed. I could feel the tension in the air, like they were both holding their breaths, waiting to see what choice I would make. To accept my mother's help, or to snub the outstretched hand because I didn't want to work with her?

It wasn't even a choice for me. There was only one option I could go with.

"So what do you know about Xenovex?" I said finally.

Her face brightened up, and I hated myself for the brief burst of warmth that bloomed in my chest after seeing her smile at my acceptance of her help.

She leaned back in her chair, thinking over what to say. Then she sat up again and looked between both of us.

"Well, I can't say much, which is as much of a disappointment for me as it is for you. I can't tell you who gave it to me, or why, but I can tell you what I know about the poison. The name itself is a recent thing, and quite modern. It was named in the 90s or the 80s, I can't quite remember."

She paused to take a sip of her tea, and then went on.

"No one alive knows how it's made, and if they do, they're keeping the secret of making it to themselves. It has been passed down from person to person, and it eventually came down to me. I have no idea what the criteria for choosing the holders of the poison are—only that they have to promise not to use it."

That doesn't mean much. People break promises all the time.

"It's odorless, but causes some color change in whatever it's added to. I'm sorry that you had to find this out the hard way, but it also kills extremely fast, usually before any sort of medical help can arrive."

I sunk further into my chair at the reminder of Diana's death. Fortunately, she changed the topic quickly.

"I do know that it's been a subject of much interest among certain circles in the scientific community and among those who know. In the underground markets it would sell for quite a lot if anyone intended to sell it off, although I can't imagine why they would do that. Also a lot of supernaturals are interested in it, though I don't know why."

Thanks, Tiana, but none of this has been actually helpful.

"What else?" I asked, before I could stop myself. My mother raised an eyebrow at me.

"What?"

I sighed, loud and irritated. "I asked what else? What else do you know? Because none of what you just told me will help me find Diana's killer."

She pursed her lips like she always did whenever she was trying not to say something she would regret or she was trying to do both.

"Charlotte…" She sighed again, trailing off. She took a deep breath and started again. "Your great-grandmother appeared to me, and if my guess is right, she'll want to speak to you too."

"So you don't know when exactly she'll be coming?"

She shook her head. "No, but I can tell you it won't be long. I know you don't want to even breathe the same air as me, but you'll have to wait for a bit for Elena."

I considered the idea. I didn't want to wait. We'd already found the Dark Stone, and all that was left was to contact the mysterious caller and see what they said. Then again, Elena Appleman might know a lot about everything I wanted to know. All in all, it was best to wait for her. The Dark Stone wasn't going anywhere, after all.

I huffed and slouched in my chair. "Fine, I'll wait. Just don't expect me to be happy about it."

13

ELENA APPLEMAN

We were doing a bit of catch-up, Detective Grey and my mother doing most of the talking. Who was I kidding—they were having a conversation with each other while I stewed in my anger over in my corner on the couch. I'd cooled down a bit as the time passed, but I still wasn't okay with my mother being in my house. How had she even gotten in?

I appreciated that they both realized I wasn't in the mood for small talk, with everything that was going on and the strained relationship with my mother. Detective Grey didn't have any such problems with her, though, and was happily telling her what his father was getting up to as an amateur ghost hunter/ghost-whisperer.

At some point Pearl sauntered out of the kitchen, where she'd been devouring the can of tuna I'd gone to put out for her when she started meowing so loudly Detective Grey and my mother could barely converse. I put out my arm and she jumped onto my arm, as I quickly brought my other arm around to support her weight before placing her on my lap.

My mother paused in the middle of the story she was telling Detective Grey about his father to stare at Pearl.

"That cat feels extremely familiar," she said. I shook my head at her. "You haven't met Pearl before?"

She waved the question away.

"It's not that," she said. "It just... this might sound strange, but that cat feels like my mother."

Detective Grey and I looked at each other. I couldn't stop the corners of my lips from lifting in a small smile.

"Well, sometimes Grandma possesses the cat, so I guess you're not completely wrong," I replied.

My mother looked shocked, for whatever reason. I was about to tell her that it wasn't the end of the world, and then I realized she wasn't even looking at me. She was looking behind me, at something that made her stiffen.

Detective Grey wasn't as shocked, but there was something definitely surprising as his eyes widened, and he too, looked behind me.

I turned around immediately. There was a woman standing in the kitchen doorway. Her hair was white and pulled back into a tight bun, and her clothes looked like something out of an 80s' magazine. The most striking thing about her, however, was the fact that I could see the white of the kitchen countertop behind her through her body.

She smiled at us, so I relaxed. She didn't seem to be malicious, and I had an inkling of just who was standing before us. It was my mother's reaction that confirmed it. She stood up from her chair and walked a few steps forward until she was standing in front of the ghost.

"Elena?"

I got to my feet too, much to Pearl's displeasure.

"That's Elena Appleman?" I looked at my mother, who nodded.

"I can speak for myself, thank you very much," Elena said. We all turned back to her, and Pearl meowed from beside me.

"Hello to you again, Tiana," the ghost said, smiling at my mother and looking as demure and fancy as a wealthy woman in her time period would look.

She turned to me and nodded, but she wasn't looking at me.

"And hello to you too, Melinda," she said to Pearl. My mother whirled round to stare at Pearl too.

"Is my mother in the cat?" she shrieked. I couldn't tell why she seemed to have such an issue with it, but thankfully, Detective Grey answered for me.

"It's kind of complicated, but yes, Melinda's the one in the cat now. She only possesses the cat when it's important, though."

My mother shook her head at him. "That doesn't really answer any of my questions, but there are more pressing issues at stake right now, aren't there?" she said, turning back to where I stood, facing the ghost who was inspecting me with such enthusiasm I was starting to get worried.

"And you must be Charlotte," Elena Appleman said. I mustered up a smile even though it felt like dragging an object out of rapidly hardening concrete.

"It's nice to meet you."

She nodded back, and then clapped her hands loudly.

"Now that the introductions are over with, let's get back to the real reason I'm here—has Tiana told you anything?"

I sneaked a glance at my mother, suddenly realizing that she might have met Elena in the flesh when she was much younger. *They certainly don't act as awkward and distant as Elena and I.* My mother shrugged.

"I told her only what you asked me to, that she might be in danger and might need my help. You didn't give me any more information, so I did my best."

The ghost nodded at her and turned back to me. "Have you accepted her help?"

"Well, yes, but I don't even know what I need her help for—"

"That's wonderful. I'll get to that now." She paused. It was weird to imagine the thought of a ghost looking unsure of themselves, but she quickly grew confident. I guessed ghosts and human beings just occupied different ends of the same spectrum, but if I wanted to be sure I'd have to ask George. I filed that thought away as something to do much, much later when all of this was done and dusted. I tuned back into the conversation.

"Well, this might be unbelievable, but please hold any questions you might have until I've finished explaining. Do you understand?" She looked between us, "us" not including Detective Grey, for whatever reason. I nodded, following the action with a "Yes" and my mother echoed my words a second later.

Elena nodded, satisfied. "You might want to be seated for this," she said. I headed back to my spot on the couch next to Pearl, starting to get frustrated at the suspense. Just tell us what it is already!

When we were all settled, she took a few steps forward that brought her into the room, and took a deep breath, something I didn't think ghosts needed to do. It must have been a subconscious action, because without even exhaling she began to speak.

"I assume we all know by now that I used to be a witch." She looked around as all of us, even Detective Grey, nodded, then went on, "Well, I can't say whether it was by choice or that I was manipulated into choosing to become one, but looking back I can't say that I regret the choice."

"How to say this? Tiana, Charlotte, even Melinda—you all inherited my genes, and of course, my magic. Meaning, of course, that you're both—"

"Witches," my mother and I said simultaneously. Pearl meowed a second later.

"Yes," Elena said with a nod. She looked at me, probably trying to gauge my reaction. I didn't know whether to apologize for a lack of the shock she'd probably expected on my face. So many things had happened since I'd come to Picklesquare that some things, like being told by the ghost of your great-grandmother that you were a witch, didn't really faze me as they should have.

There was also the fact that I had no idea what being a witch even entailed, so I didn't know whether to be excited or to be disgusted. All I knew was from books and movies, and there were so many different interpretations of witches. Would I turn green and have numerous warts all over my face while I stirred the bones of children in a large cauldron? Would I have to move into the forest and live in a cottage while swanning around in black robes and bare feet?

"Oh," was all I could muster. My mother gave me an affronted look.

"'Oh'? Is that all you have to say?" she asked. I shrugged. *Why is she taking it so personally?*

Elena saved me from having to answer. "There's nothing wrong with not being overly enthused about this revelation, Tiana. Leave the girl alone."

It felt strange to be called a girl after so many years, but I supposed I was indeed a girl compared to Elena.

"And it's not like she has her powers at the moment either, so there's no use in getting excited about the revelation."

"What do you mean I don't have my powers?" I had to ask. "But you just said—"

"I know what I said, Charlotte," Elena replied sternly. "Your powers are dormant, however, which is one of the reasons I asked Tiana to come to Picklesquare."

I glanced at my mother, confused.

"What do you mean? What does her presence here have to do with anything?" I asked.

Elena shook her head. "I can't tell you why, because I don't know the answer myself, but her presence near you is a crucial factor in waking up your powers. It's probably due to the magic being inherited, but I can't give you any other reason as to why."

I sighed and leaned back on the couch. Wonderful. I was now stuck with my mother, who I very much did not want to see, just so I could acquire the magic that I was already supposed to have. It made a little sense to me that my powers were dormant because my mother hadn't been in my life for some time—another thing to be angry at her for.

"So what now? Wait, why do I even need magic? I've gotten this far without it, and I ended up fine at the end."

Elena shook her head at me. "Sadly, that's not the case this time. You'll need all the help you can get right now, especially since you're dealing with the Dark Stone."

I sat up, and out of the corner of my eye, I noticed Detective Grey doing the same thing.

"What do you mean?" For some reason, my heartbeat had gotten faster. I wasn't sure I liked where Elena was going with her words.

She sighed. "I don't know if you've felt it, though I doubt that you have, but there is something extremely unsettling about that maze and the Dark Stone within it. It practically oozes darkness—the kind you don't want to be in alone and without a source of light, not the comfortable darkness."

I wasn't convinced. "And why hasn't anyone, even you, felt it before now? From what you're saying, people should have been staying away from the house or the maze, rather. Even people who aren't aware of the supernatural can feel these things sometimes."

She nodded. "Yes, you're quite right. However, the reason no one felt it all this time was because the maze was sealed shut. Now it's been opened, and the evil presence in it has leaked its aura. It's going to attract a lot of bad things, and you have to be prepared."

I stared at her. "What, like the end of the world? A literal Armageddon?"

She nodded gravely, and the worst part was that I believed her.

"It could mean the end of just Picklesquare if we're lucky. If we're not so lucky, maybe the end of the country or the state. If we have really bad luck; however, it could mean the end of the world as we know it."

There was a stunned silence as we tried to process her words.

"Of course," she added after shocking us into silence, "I could just be overreacting, and making a mountain out of a molehill. Who knows?"

I looked at my mother and Detective Grey. *Were things really that bad now that we'd opened the maze?*

14

THE DARK STONE

I looked at Detective Grey, who looked back at me. I turned back to Elena.

"What do you mean? What's going to happen?" I needed more clarification before I worked myself into a panic over what might turn out to be nothing at all in the end.

My great-grandmother shook her head.

"There's no way to explain it, or to give you all the details—I barely even have any, but I will tell you what I know. You're looking for the Dark Stone, aren't you?"

I nodded. "Someone was nice enough to offer me a way to bring Diana back to life if I brought them the Dark Stone."

She shook her head wildly almost as the last word left my mouth. My mother did the same thing, adding, "And you thought that was safe to do?" to the clear disappointment on her face.

"I wouldn't advise you to do that," she said. "Who knows whether this is going to backfire on you or not, and if it does, you might not be so pleased with the outcome."

I shrugged. "What else could I do? Whoever it was made the deal nearly impossible to refuse by making it possible for me to possibly see and speak to my dead friend again. Of course, I would choose Diana over the Dark Stone."

"An admirable quality in a friend, but for the rest of us we have to worry about putting the Dark Stone in the wrong hands."

My mother looked at me, worried. "Are you sure you won't give up your search? We don't know who this person is or what their plans are for the Dark Stone—"

"When I get to that bridge I'll cross it," I cut in, holding up one hand to stop the questions I knew would be coming. "I would like to know what they're going to do, but right now all I need to do is get my hands on it. I'll think about whether this person is being genuine or not after I have something to bargain with."

My mother obviously wasn't satisfied with that, but Elena held up a hand to stop her from saying what was on her mind.

"Leave it alone, Tiana. You can tell she already had her heart set on it, so there's no point wasting your breath. Now, what was I going to say before we took that little detour?"

Detective Grey piped up. "You were going to tell us about the 'dark, evil presence' you felt."

She nodded at him. "Thank you, my dear. Well, I can't exactly explain it to you in detail. All I can say is that this presence is not concrete or something you can interact with to take it out of the equation. All you can do is be aware of it, and to be prepared for anything that could happen."

I shared a glance with Detective Grey. We weren't new to situations like that. We'd just recently emerged from a maze that had thrown so many unexpected occurrences at us. We could handle it.

"It should not be much of a surprise to you that this presence I've felt is related to the Dark Stone. I could even go as far as saying that the Dark Stone is the reason for this presence, another reason for you to take every and any precautionary measures when you finally get a hold of it."

I nodded. Parts of it made sense, like how the dark presence might be due to the Dark Stone existing. Other parts were not so clear, however. What did she mean by saying we had to be careful?

"Does the Dark Stone place a curse on whoever holds or uses it?"

She fixed her gaze on me. "Why do you ask?"

I shrugged. "I'm wondering why you say it's so dangerous."

She sighed. "To make you understand fully, I must go back to the beginning of everything—when the Dark Stone was created."

I sat up straighter and leaned forward, every other person in the room doing the same as my great-grandmother launched into her story.

"We don't know how long ago this was, but it was more than six or seven centuries ago. There was a quite charismatic and powerful man, who, while he had a good deal of prestige in the town where he lived, also held a position of power in the supernatural community as one of the top warlocks of his generation. He had a fiercely loyal group of followers who waited on him day and night and treated him like he could do no wrong. In return, he taught them more than they would ever learn by themselves, although he kept a few secrets close to his chest.

"You can see how this sort of thing could go wrong, as it soon became a cult. Not all of them were pleased at having to literally worship a fellow human being, and they broke off from the cult to become their own thing. Let's put them to the side for now. They'll come up much later. So this warlock and his followers left the town and made their base in the forest at the outskirts of the town. The people thought it was strange, but as long as the cultists kept to themselves no one bothered them."

She paused. "That is, until people began to go missing after wandering too close to the forest or away from their companions. At first it wasn't even humans going missing, just livestock and the occasional pet that strayed too far. The townspeople blamed the predators in the forest. Then travelers to the village, merchants who used to pass through the village at certain times in the year or just relatives of the town's inhabitants, started to go missing also. They'd set off on a journey, but would never reach their destination. Inquiries made would always reveal that the travelers went missing halfway between the town five miles away and the town our story takes place in. Even the townspeople who left weren't spared, with a notable case of an entire family emigrating from the town ending up missing.

"So no one came in, and no one went out... except the cultists. People thought it was weird, but shrugged it off. Suspicions grew, though, and finally, after twenty children were snatched up, the townspeople finally pointed the finger at the cult."

I wondered how all of this was related to the Dark Stone. *I guess I am about to find out.*

"So the mayor called a meeting and invited the leader of the cult. They met at the town square, with all the villagers in attendance and the cult leader flanked by some of his members. The people hurled insults at the cultists, and they were very close to grabbing them and beating them up.

"Then, the warlock got to his feet and began to chant. The people could not move their bodies, but they could move their mouths, and soon the air was filled with frightened screams and angry shouting. The warlock did not even bat an eye, but his followers got to their feet and scattered, each of them taking a cardinal direction and standing behind the people who had gathered."

I wasn't sure I liked where this was going.

"Then he began to chant again, and as he chanted his followers stepped forward, bringing out sharp daggers they'd hidden in their strange clothes. The townspeople screamed and begged and threatened them, but they couldn't move to even resist as the cultists went around striking down the people with their daggers. By the end of it all, the ground in the town square was dyed red, and the warlock was still chanting."

She paused, her expression grim. "When he finally ended his chant, the blood on the ground flowed into a large sphere at his feet, leaving the ground clean again, like there hadn't been blood on it just seconds ago. The sphere morphed into what we now call the Dark Stone."

I sat back in my seat, my mind spinning. It was starting to make a lot of sense now.

"He took his prize and his followers and disappeared back into the forest, but unknown to him someone had witnessed the entire thing, a woman who was lying ill in bed and couldn't get to the village square on time for the meeting. Somehow this woman managed to escape the village and the so-called curse that plagued the route from the town, but no one believed her when she told her story. She was about to give up until one of the people who had left the cult heard it, and with the rest of his group, he followed the woman back to the town.

"I've already said so much that going into more detail would be a waste of time, but all you need to know is that the sacrifices and in turn, the Dark Stone, were crucial to the increasing power and ambition of the warlock. He wanted to be a true god, to rule the world, and creating an item as powerful as the Dark Stone that could do things like warp reality was just step one."

"Wait, did you just say the Dark Stone can warp reality?" I echoed.

She nodded. "It can, and it can do even more than that. No one is sure, but the various realities within the maze might be due to the Dark Stone's presence."

She waited for a moment, but no one else had any questions, so she went on.

"This group, now known by the title of Order of Oscuros—you recognize the name, then?" She turned to me, raising an eyebrow at my now wide eyes.

"Yes, uh, we learned a little about it in the maze. They were the ones who made you a witch?"

She nodded. "Yes. And the name of the cult is the Order of the Sun. Both groups are still very much active, both with different goals and different means of achieving those goals. My parents were members, so that's how I know all that I know."

"And what happened between the Order of the Sun and the other Order?" Detective Grey asked.

She smiled at him. "The Order of Oscuros won, of course. Things might have been very different for all of us if they hadn't. They managed to weaken the self-proclaimed Dark Lord enough to take the Dark Stone from him. Foolishly, he'd bound the object to his soul, so when they sealed it he slipped into a sleep none of his followers could wake him up from. Unfortunately, some of the Sun members escaped, but Oscuros rounded up everyone they could. Then they left the area and took the Dark Lord's body and the Dark Stone to another place, where they created an underground labyrinth and sealed the Dark Stone and his body at the center of the maze."

Something had been niggling at me. "Why didn't they just bury him somewhere else, instead of close to the Dark Stone? Isn't that dangerous?"

Elena shook her head. "He didn't die, remember? He's been in a deep sleep ever since, and the only thing that can bring him back to consciousness again is the Dark Stone. I don't know exactly how it could wake him up, which is why you should be extremely careful in dealing with the Dark Stone when you eventually find it. It would be a disaster of colossal proportions if he woke up, and even worse, if you were unable to protect yourself, seeing as your powers are still dormant."

After she stopped speaking, the room was quiet. What could we say? I'd been aware that the maze had an element of danger to it, but now I was learning that the object of my search was the key to releasing a powerful centuries-old evil man.

I shook the fear off. *I just have to be careful, won't I? I can't give up, not now that we were nearly at the end. Nothing is going to make me change my mind.*

15

GIRL WITH THE TATTOO

"What are you going to do now?" Tiana asked, looking between Detective Grey and me.

He glanced at me, and I gave him a determined look.

"What else? We have to go back in the maze. I'm pretty sure we've already found the Dark Stone, and Rachel and Diana are still down there, waiting for us. I don't know what we'll do about the person who called me and promised to revive Diana in exchange for the Stone, but like I said before, I'll think about it when it happens."

Tiana frowned at me, but she didn't say anything. I knew what she was thinking – that I was gambling on a chance that someone I couldn't even vouch for would not end up being a member of the Order of the Sun trying to revive their slumbering master, and that they could even revive Diana in the first place.

She would be surprised if she knew I was thinking the same thing. At this point it was clear to me that I couldn't give up the Dark Stone to just anyone, moreover, I couldn't trust the mysterious person who'd reached out to me. Mysteriously, they'd known that I was looking for the Dark Stone, which was impossible unless they were close to me or they'd overheard Detective Grey and me talking about it, but I couldn't think of anyone who fit both criteria.

I was also starting to doubt that whoever it was could actually bring Diana back to life, like they'd promised. Even worse was the disquieting thought that a success might not make me happy. What if it ended up like a monkey's paw situation? There were many ways to revive Diana, and many ways the promise could be twisted.

I couldn't just give up though, not after I'd gotten so far. I pushed the thoughts away and squared my shoulders.

"It's been very nice to meet you, Elena," I said, not glancing at my mother, "but we have to go back now. Rachel and Diana are waiting for us."

She nodded. "Good luck with your endeavors. I hope that things work out for all of you–"

"I'm sorry to interrupt, but I just remembered something very important," Tiana said, speaking quickly in excitement. She looked at me. "I think you'll want to hear this, Charlotte."

I raised an eyebrow. What did she have to say that was so important? I nodded at her anyway, signaling her to continue.

"It's about the Xenovex," she said, and I was instantly hooked.

"What about it?"

"Well, it's locked up in my lab, right? Right outside the lab are my offices. I see regular humans in the outer one and supernatural ones in the inner one. Well, I was on the last of my patients for the day, which was a young woman about Charlotte's age or a bit younger with a really strange tattoo on her wrist. Something about that tattoo just pulled at something in my mind, like I'd seen it before but I couldn't remember what it meant. Then I got a call and had to step out for a bit. Mind you, I attended to her in the outer office, and left the office completely for a bit. The lab was locked though, so I wasn't worried about anyone getting in."

She stopped to catch her breath, and then went on. "The issue was, when I got back, the person I was treating was nowhere to be found. I asked the receptionist if she'd left while I was gone, but she said she hadn't stepped out of the room at all. It was possible that she'd been too engrossed in her work to see the girl with the tattoo walk past, so I went out of the office to the front desk of the building that houses my office. They hadn't seen her either. Just as I walked back into my office, thinking she'd already left, who do I see leaving my inner offices but this young woman?"

Detective Grey and I exchanged looks.

"She said she'd been looking for the bathroom, but I doubt she was being completely honest. The toilets are clearly marked and are off a small corridor to the right of the entrance. Nothing was missing when I checked my office, though, but the door of the inner office was unlocked, and I am one hundred percent sure I'd locked it. I didn't even connect it to discovering the Xenovex missing three days later, but knowing what I know now I wonder if she took it..."

Something occurred to me and I gasped. "Wait, what did the tattoo look like?"

She frowned and squinted. "I can't remember–it wasn't a really large tattoo, just on the inside of the wrist, and it was red."

I lifted my eyebrows. My heart rate had increased, and as I jumped out of my seat and ran to the large table behind the couch I could hear people getting to their feet.

"Charlotte? What's going on? What are you looking for?" Detective Grey asked as he rushed to stand behind me. I grabbed a small notepad off the table and nearly upturned the entire contents of the table in my search for a pen I could use. I couldn't explain it to him just yet, but if it was what I was thinking–

I let out a victorious yell as I finally found a pencil somewhere in the numerous objects I'd decorated the table with. Quickly, I tore out a sheet of paper from the notepad, placed it on top of the pad and began to draw. I drew two arcs intersecting in the middle, like someone had taken a Venn diagram of two interlocking circles and cut out the bottom half, leaving only the top half. The arcs were surrounded by lines going out from them like sun rays, and the final stroke was a horizontal line under the whole thing.

When I was done I dropped everything except the paper and stomped over to my mother, who looked bewildered at everything that was happening.

"Charlotte, is everything alright–?"

I shoved the paper into her face.

"Is this the tattoo you saw?" I asked, my heart beating in my ears. She gave me a look, leaned back and snatched the paper out of my grasp before looking at it.

I watched as instant recognition came onto her face and she looked up at me, confused.

"Yes, that's the tattoo. But how did you know?"

I didn't answer. I'd already sunk back into my seat, bending over my knees to face the floor, leaning my elbows on my knees. I blinked away the hot tears coming into my eyes. One of them escaped, despite my efforts to keep it in my eyes, and dropped onto the pale carpet beneath my feet. A small circle in the carpet grew darker, and I wondered if that was some sort of metaphor about the way my life was going.

There was a cool hand on my shoulder. I knew who it was immediately – no other person in the room had such calloused palms.

"Charlotte? Is everything alright?" he asked quietly. I shook my head. I didn't want to do anything at all, except go back to my room, curl up in bed under a blanket and sleep, and pretend someone else had all these problems for a bit. Someone who wasn't me.

"Well then, what's the problem?"

I sniffed, wiped my eyes and finally looked up. I didn't look at Detective Grey. I didn't want to see the sympathy in his eyes, because I would just break down sobbing. What I needed now was to solve the problem, and taking time off to cry about it wasn't part of my plans. There was no time for that.

Instead I looked at my mother, who was still staring at the paper I'd handed her. I thought about the pain I'd felt when she left me behind, and how it had eventually transformed into anger when I realized she wouldn't be coming back for me. I let the anger flow through me until I felt I would soon start seeing red, and then I turned to Detective Grey.

"I'm fine, I just realized something," I told him. He didn't look reassured by my words.

"What is it?" he asked. Just as I was about to answer, Tiana spoke up instead.

"Hey... I know where I've seen this before."

I turned to her, slightly irritated at the unintentional interruption.

"What is it? Where's it from?" Detective Grey asked before I could.

She tapped the paper. "This? I remember now that it had some stupid name... yes, that's it! They called it the 'Mark of the Dark,' if you can believe that."

Elena snapped to attention at that. "The Mark of the Dark, you say?" She'd been floating near the kitchen, but she came closer, up to my mother. Tiana held up the paper with the symbol I'd drawn on it for her to look at it. She frowned at it and floated back to her spot near the kitchen.

"What does it mean?" Detective Grey asked again.

Tiana looked at Elena, who sighed and shook her head.

"It's a sign of belonging to the Order of the Sun."

I shot up from my seat at her words. That wasn't possible.

"You're serious?" I asked. I was grasping at straws at that point, hoping for a miracle when I knew there was going to be none.

"Of course I am," Elena sounded affronted. "Why would I joke about something so important? And why are you going pale?"

I shook my head frantically. There was no time to worry about me. We had to get back down into the maze.

"We have to go down now," I said to Detective Grey, grabbing his arm and pulling him towards the door. Rather, I tried to. He didn't budge, giving me a stern frown instead and shaking his head at me.

"Charlotte, what's going on? You haven't told us anything at all."

I stopped and turned to them. They watched me with concerned looks on their faces, like I'd suddenly gone insane.

I took a deep breath and did my best to explain using the least amount of words I could.

"That tattoo I drew? The one Elena said was the Mark of the Dark?"

They all nodded.

"Yes, well, Rachel has that same tattoo on her wrist! And if I'm correct, she's the one who stole the last of the Xenovex and poisoned Diana's tea."

Detective Grey went white as the implications of my accusation dawned on him.

"Are you sure about this, Charlotte?" he asked. I guessed he didn't want to believe it either.

I shivered. "We'll know when we get down there again, won't we?"

Elena sighed. "So this means that this Rachel person is a member of the Order of the Sun?"

I nodded in agreement. "It gets even worse, if you can believe it," I said with a grim smile.

Elena frowned. "What do you mean?"

I slumped my shoulders. "Rachel invited herself on our journey through the maze. I didn't suspect a thing, so I let her come along. But just before we came up here, we found the Dark Stone."

If a ghost could blanch, Elena would have been as white as a sheet of paper. Instead she had a look of horror on her face.

"Oh no..."

Detective Grey nodded soberly. "And from what you've told us, the body of the Sun's leader is down there, with the Dark Stone."

"And she now has the Dark Stone, her master, and Diana in her possession. She can resurrect him anytime she wants," I added.

"Like I said before, we need to go. Now."

16

BACK INTO THE MAZE

"It's not your fault, Charlotte," Detective Grey whispered as we hurried to the door that would take us back into the maze. "You didn't want her to come in the first place."

"And yet she's down there with Diana's ghost," I snapped, feeling bad almost immediately after I said it. He was trying to make me feel better, even though he was as worried as I was. *There is no need to take out my frustrations on him...*

I sighed. "I'm sorry."

He placed his hand on my shoulder as we stopped in front of the door. "It's okay, Charlotte. Don't beat yourself up about it, you've apologized already, and we all make mistakes, don't we?"

I missed the warmth of his hand when he took it off my shoulder to open the door, but I quickly buried that thought, and what it meant that I wanted his hand back on my body. There were more important things to think about at that moment.

Behind us, my mother and Elena caught up just as he opened the door.

"Be careful," Elena said, looking as worried as Tiana. "I might not know who this Rachel is, but if she's a member of the Order of the Sun then she's very dangerous."

"Exactly," my mother chimed in. "Don't put yourself at risk when you don't need to. Diana's already dead, but you're still alive."

I swiveled my head to face her so quickly I felt like my neck should've snapped from the force of it.

"Excuse you?" I hissed. How dare she?

"Charlotte, we don't have the time for this, please."

I shared one last glance with my mother, who looked unapologetic. Then I nodded at Detective Grey, hovering near the door, and stepped through it. I wasn't sure it was going to work initially, but the moment my foot hit the ground on the other side I was back in that dark, empty room.

I stared as Detective Grey came after me. I heard the door close behind him, and he whispered a curse under his breath, one that I agreed with immensely.

We were in deep and serious trouble.

Where there had only been empty space before we'd left the room, now hooded strangers in dark robes stood in a crescent across from us. The pointed ends of the crescent came quite close to where we stood, and the people at the tip of the crescent on either side even took a step sideways, bringing them closer to us and making me feel less safe than I'd been when I first stepped in.

At the center of the room, where the plinth that housed the Dark Stone stood, was Rachel, cradling the Stone in her palms and giving us a triumphant and irritating smirk. She stood in the center in front of the crescent so that it looked like she was the focal point of the room. And she was, stepping forward to greet us with a disdainful scoff.

"Charlotte! Detective Grey! How nice of you two to join me again. I brought some friends, hope you don't mind."

I glared at her, hating that that was the only thing I could do. Another thing that worried me was how I couldn't see Diana or what was left of her anywhere.

"What is this? Who are all these people? And where is Diana?" I had more questions, like had these strangers been in the maze all along, because I didn't think we'd spent that much time in my house, and how could she betray us like that? Those questions didn't need urgent answers though, so I left them alone.

She smiled at me. It was the same smile she'd always had, but now, somehow, it felt malevolent, not full of joy like it used to be. It felt like she was laughing at a joke only she knew the punchline to, and even worse, I was sure I was the butt of said joke.

"Oh, her?" She turned to her "friends" who stood near the other door, the one leading to the rest of the maze, and said, "Bring the body in."

I didn't have time to puzzle out what it meant, I found out quickly. They nodded, their high hoods dipping almost comically with the movement, and left the room, coming back in seconds later carrying a long burden between them. They brought their burden to the center of the room and laid it down, rather roughly, at Rachel's feet.

"Show them," she said softly, still smiling.

One of them bent again and dramatically uncovered the brown cloth that covered the... body. I looked down at the pale face of my best friend and then looked into Rachel's amused eyes. What was so funny?

"How dare you?"

What was the purpose of bringing Diana's body down here? To laugh at our expense and make jokes out of our grief?

Detective Grey stepped forward to stand beside me. I didn't look away from Rachel's smug face, but I could hear the forced calm in his voice.

"What about Daya and—"

Rachel interrupted. I was beginning to see that she loved to hear herself speak.

"Her little boyfriend? What was his name again... James? John? Whatever." She snickered, and for some reason, the rest of them did too. It was horrible to hear the laughter and feel that something was wrong at the same time. I stepped forward.

"What did you do to them?" I demanded.

She rolled her eyes. "Alright, settle down." The laughter stopped as abruptly as it had started. "Your friends are fine, just asleep for now."

I couldn't tell if that meant that they were unconscious or actually asleep, but strangely I believed her when she said they were fine. There was no reason for her to lie to us. She'd gotten what she wanted, and now she could gloat all she wanted.

She clapped her hands sharply, bringing our attention back to her.

"Yes, I have no idea if I've said this already, but I'm going to say it again. Welcome to the final act. Everything before this has been for the sole purpose of this moment. And we're finally here! Isn't that exciting? Are you not excited?"

I shook my head, even though her words were *clearly* meant for her fellow cultists. They rumbled in agreement and one person went as far as clapping, although they stopped immediately when no one joined them.

"What do you want with us?" Detective Grey asked. I glanced at him. His jaw was set, and he was clenching and unclenching his fists.

Rachel shrugged. "I've already told Charlotte what I wanted from her, but it's no issue at all for me to go over it again."

Detective Grey glanced at me and raised an eyebrow. I shook my head in response. I couldn't remember Rachel ever coming to me with a request. What was she talking about? She huffed at our blank stares and opened her mouth to explain.

"Somehow Charlotte is the key to raising our Dark Lord," she paused and closed her eyes, shuddering at the mention of their leader like several of the robed forms around us, then went on, "and I said it before, didn't I? I'll revive Diana in exchange for the Dark Lord's awakening."

Beside me, I heard a hitched breath, but my gasp was much louder.

"You're the unknown caller!"

Rachel rolled her eyes at me.

"I am. Do you want a prize or something?"

I gritted my teeth and told myself to be polite, even though I wanted to tackle that smug face to the ground and squeeze her neck until her eyes popped out of their sockets.

"If you can revive Diana, why not just revive the Dark Lord?" I asked.

She scoffed. "Yeah, if I could, I wouldn't need you, would I? Stop wasting my time. Will you do it or not?" She paused and looked over her shoulder at Diana's corpse.

"Although I must warn you that declining would mean you would no longer get to see your precious Diana and be quick about it. The more you delay, the faster her body decomposes. Bringing her back to life is useless if she's nothing but a skeleton in the end. I hope you know that."

"How do I know you'll keep to your end of the bargain? You already have the Dark Stone. Nothing is stopping you from just getting rid of us after I've done what you wanted," I countered. My argument was full of holes, but I couldn't think of any other way to stall her while I thought about it.

Rachel snorted loudly and sneered.

"Look, if I could do it myself, I wouldn't have gone to all the trouble of stealing the Xenovex and stalking you two until I could use the poison. Don't flatter yourself. You're not that important. And will you just make a decision? Time is ticking, and I'd like to be out of this stupid maze as soon as possible."

I turned to Detective Grey, even though I already knew what he would say: Don't do it, Charlotte. He was like the angel on my shoulder, and like most people, I never really listened to the angel on my shoulder.

"Don't do it, Charlotte. You might end up regretting it."

I shook my head. "I won't."

"How can you be so sure?" He leaned down to whisper in such a low tone that I had to strain to hear him. "We don't know these people. They can say one thing and do another. You really want to release such a threat into the world?"

"Tick-tock!" Rachel called out. "I'm starting to run out of patience here."

"Do you want to lose Diana forever?" I hissed at Detective Grey.

He looked stricken at the thought. "No," he said after a brief silence. "I don't. But people die, Charlotte. We can't really change that."

I glared at him. "Well this time I can, and I will. Watch me."

I turned away from him and back to Rachel. Some part of me wondered if I was doing the right thing by making a deal with Diana's killer. I had Detective Grey on my side. If we tried we could probably build a case against Rachel and send her to prison.

On the other hand, I missed Diana intensely. I'd lost one friend before. I wasn't going to lose another, not when I could do something about it this time.

I straightened up and looked Rachel in the eye.

"I've made my decision," I said, noting out of the corner of my eye the way Detective Grey tensed. I wondered how he knew me so well, that he knew what I was going to choose. Either way, I wasn't changing my mind, no matter what anyone, even Diana, thought.

17

THE DARK LORD

"I'll do it."

Detective Grey whirled on me, giving me a disapproving look.

"Charlotte!"

"What?" I snapped. He didn't need to say anything. I wasn't a child, I knew the repercussions of my actions, and I wasn't going to apologize for anything.

"Nothing," he sighed. "Do what you want."

I was hurt deep down by the dismissal in his tone, but that wasn't going to stop me. My mind was made up, and if this is what I had to do to get Diana back, I would do it.

"Wonderful!" Rachel grinned. She motioned to the people standing at the tip of the crescent in which the cultists were arranged, gesturing with her head at Detective Grey beside me. "Hold him down."

"Wait, what are you doing?" I started to protest, but Rachel held up a hand, stopping me from speaking further.

"Don't worry about your boyfriend, Charlotte. We're just making sure he doesn't interfere," she explained as the two cultists grabbed Detective Grey's arms, one on each side, and pulled him to the back of the room. He gave me a reassuring look as they pulled him away, and I felt even worse. Just minutes before I had been angry with him for daring to suggest that maybe I wasn't doing the right thing, but now he wasn't even holding anything against me, even though I was the reason he was being manhandled like a prisoner.

"Hey, eyes on me," Rachel barked, stepping forward and snapping her fingers in my face. I returned my gaze to her, glaring at her. She only smirked in return.

"Great. Now that you're focused again, here," she said, dropping the Dark Stone into my hands so suddenly I had to scramble not to drop it. I didn't want to think of what would happen if I'd actually let it fall and the Stone broke. Rachel looked worried as I fumbled the Stone in my hands but when I was finally clutching it safely in my hands she sneered at me.

"Way to go, Charlotte. I hope you know that Stone is more precious than your life."

I glared at her and left it at that. "So what do I do now?" I asked. She shrugged.

"I don't know. You're the one with the magic. Figure it out. But do it fast, because we can't sit around waiting for you."

I sighed. I shouldn't have been surprised that Rachel was of no help. I looked down at the Stone in my hands. Maybe if I focused on it, something would happen?

It was the only idea I had at the moment, so I did just that, closing my eyes and using all my mental energy to focus on the sphere in my hands. I thought about how it felt, the cool surface of the Stone contrasting with the warmth and sweat on my palms, the faint warmth I could feel that radiated from inside the Stone, how it grew hotter and hotter, and how, even though my eyes were closed, I could see it clearly in my mind's eye.

I tried to open my eyes, starting to feel uncomfortable with the sensations I was feeling, but my eyelids felt heavy and hard to pull apart, like they'd been glued shut. I tried to speak, but like my eyelids, my lips stayed closed.

Calm down.

Who said that? Just then I noticed how quiet everything was around me. I hadn't taken much notice of the sounds in the room before then, but it was obvious now. There was no shifting of feet against the floor, and I could no longer hear that one person who was breathing loudly.

Something was up, and I didn't like it. The tension in the air was so thick I felt like I could reach out and touch it, that is, if I could even move my arms. I tried and found, to no surprise, that I couldn't.

I couldn't even twitch a finger, and the Stone in my palms seemed to get heavier and heavier.

Charlotte Miller, is it?

The voice came again. It sounded masculine, deep and amused.

Who are you? I thought, realizing that I wasn't actually hearing the voice in my ears. It was just in my thoughts. That was scarier than hearing a voice I couldn't see.

I'm not scary. Don't worry. The voice came again, but I would be a fool to feel reassured. There was an undertone of malice that curled around the words the voice said. I had a feeling this voice didn't have the best intentions for me.

Can you read my mind? I thought again. If whoever this was could, well, that proved to be even scarier.

Only the surface thoughts, the voice said, slick as oil. *It's been a long time since I've communicated with another human being,* the voice said again. *Pardon me if I make any errors.*

It's fine, I replied hurriedly. I got the sense that the voice was starting to get impatient, so it was best if we both went to the reason I was even here in the first place.

Are you the leader of the Order of the Sun? I asked, thinking better of calling him the Dark Lord to his face. I didn't want him to get offended, especially since there was no way I could currently see to get myself out of this predicament.

I am, came the reply. He sounded pleased about it. *And you are here to ensure my return to the world, yes?*

I agreed. *Well, yes, but I don't know how,* I admitted, feeling small and stupid. I only recently learned I had magic. I felt like I should apologize, but that would be going too far. I didn't owe him anything, and I wasn't freeing him of my own will.

That is not an issue, the voice said again. I was starting to feel uncomfortable with having this voice in my head. It felt like a poisonous snake was slowly slithering up my back and around my shoulders, and I was tense all the while, wondering when it was going to strike.

I can guide you, he continued. *All you have to do is say my name.*

I raised a mental eyebrow. Was it really that easy?

My doubt must have reached him, because he responded, trying to remove my doubt. *It will be easy for you,* he said, *because you have power. A lot of it, in fact. I'm almost jealous.*

Somehow I didn't feel flattered. It was an interesting piece of information though. *How can you tell?*

I got the feeling that he was shrugging, and immediately after he replied, I could feel it. *The more one is acquainted with magic, the more they'll be able to feel these things. I might have been asleep for a long time but my senses are still as sharp as ever.*

Alright. So how do I do this?

Why so hurried? We still have some time. Let's discuss.

I was confused at his response. I'd felt his impatience not too long ago, and now he wanted to discuss? The crazy thing was, I didn't think he was lying about wanting to talk. He'd been impatient before, but now he wasn't. *What made him change his mind?*

Don't you want to be alive again?

There was a dark chuckle. *I've been asleep for so long, what is a few more minutes in the grand scheme of things? Don't worry your pretty little head over me. We'll get to that in time.*

I rankled at the phrase but held back my irritation. *What do you want to talk about?* I asked instead, truly curious.

You.

Me?

You, yes. You're very powerful, my dear. Imagine how much more powerful you'll be with the proper training and resources.

You're offering to teach me? I could hardly believe what I was hearing. Crazy things happened to me regularly, but this was the most surprised I'd ever been.

Is it so surprising? You have talent. It would be a waste not to nurture it. Become my apprentice, the voice offered. *We could do marvelous things together.*

I was quiet for a while, thinking it over. If this voice was telling the truth (and he sounded sincere, although that could be a lie as well), then I had the potential to become very powerful. I wouldn't need to wait for someone to rescue me all the time. I wouldn't have to rely on

Pearl to get myself out of trouble. I could do everything myself, and finally be independent and not so helpless anymore. The thought of it was enticing.

On the other hand, I was speaking to a dark lord. He'd tried to enslave the world and had gotten punished for it. What were the chances that he wouldn't try the same thing on me too, knowing even more than I did? If he wanted to lead me astray I wouldn't know.

We can rule the world together, the voice said again, probably getting tired of allowing me to contemplate my options. *I can feel that you're not one to sit back and let things just happen to you. You would be much happier being in control of your life, wouldn't you?*

I would, I replied, and it was the truth.

Excellent. Join me, and you'll be doing exactly that. The world will react to you, and not the other way round. You can even have power over life and death.

My mental ears perked up at that. *Really?* I said doubtfully. Rachel had said Diana would be resurrected if I did what she wanted, but I was starting to think she'd been lying about it.

The voice scoffed. *Rachel? She's devoted to me, which is a point in her favor, but she lacks the power to do even that. Unlike you.*

Can I bring Diana back?

No, not now. Before I could deflate in disappointment, the voice added, *But I can. You would be able to do it eventually, provided you had the training and knowledge, but right now, only I can do it.*

I wasn't going to lie to myself and say the offer didn't faze me. It was enticing, the thought of being so powerful that I could change the world. Then I thought about Diana and Detective Grey. I'd disappointed Detective Grey once already. I wasn't going to do it a second time. There was nothing at stake here and all I had to do was say no.

I did just that, framing it as subtly as I could instead of outrightly rejecting the voice's offer.

How do I wake you?

You don't want to work with me? There was a faint note of surprise in the voice like he had never considered that I would reject his offer.

I don't, I confirmed. *I just want my friend back.*

You will regret this, he warned. I shrugged inwardly. I might, but at that moment I didn't, and that was enough for me.

How do I wake you? I asked again.

His voice was angrier now, but it wasn't raised, just colder. *Very well. All you have to do is say my name.*

I couldn't hide my surprise. *That's all?*

That is all, the voice confirmed. *Without being prompted,* he explained. *You already hold the Stone housing my soul in your hands. You also have sufficient power to return my soul to my body, though you are untrained. All I have to do is use your power and work the spell that will return me to my body. That is all.*

And I won't get hurt? I asked, not caring whether the question made him angrier. We'd already broken the bridge between us. I doubted he would be nicer to me after I'd rejected him.

You are only acting as a conduit for my spell. It cannot hurt you.

And you promise you'll bring Diana back to life?

There was a deep sigh. *I promise.*

Well, I couldn't do anything but go along with it and hope he would keep his promise. *What's your name?*

The word echoed in my head, and I felt free to move again. I spoke the word.

"Zalazar."

Then a wave of energy rushed through me, and I fell to the ground, still clutching the Stone.

18

Awakening

I opened my eyes after what felt like an eternity, only to find myself in the same position I'd been in when I closed my eyes. I was still on the floor, the Dark Stone in my hand. Around me the cultists seemed agitated and restless, Rachel even coming up to me to hover over me.

"Well?" she demanded, just as there was a loud crack. All eyes in the room went down to the now cracked Stone in my hands, watching as another line tore through the Stone with another sharp crack.

"What's happening? What did you do?" Rachel hissed, grabbing my shoulders and digging into them with her sharp fingernails. I winced and tried to shake her off.

"Let go! It's working, that's all," I yelled. She clearly didn't believe me, as she didn't ease up but dug her nails in harder.

I lifted one hand to pry her fingers off my shoulder, shifting the halves of the Dark Stone into my other hand. Just as I grabbed her hand on my left shoulder a burst of energy erupted from the Stone in my hand, so hot that I had to drop the pieces of the Stone or get burned. Even with that, my palms had turned red, and I suspected I might have to put some ointment on my palm when I got home. If I ever made it back home.

The energy swept through the room in a large wave that made the walls shake, and an invisible wind blew in the room. Some of the cultists' hoods were blown off, and I caught a glimpse of one face before they quickly hid their faces again. I didn't recognize the person, though I committed their features to memory, in case I ever encountered them again.

The energy, if I could call it that, grew thicker and more powerful until we were all holding onto the walls or each other not to get blown away. Everyone's hoods were off now, but nobody cared in the face of probable destruction. The energy had turned into a swirling mass of darkness hovering over the plinth in the center of the room, and as we watched it descended on the plinth slowly.

The closer it got to the plinth, the more pressure we felt. We shifted back, Rachel doing me the favor of dragging me with her to the walls, until everyone was pressed against the walls alongside us. It must have been a funny sight, Detective Grey and me being the only normally dressed people in a room full of people dressed in black robes, each of us pressed against the wall like we wanted to sink into it and holding hands with the people on either side of us.

We held our breaths as it got harder to breathe due to the pressure, and finally, with surprising speed, the energy fell through the plinth and into the outlined rectangle under the plinth, turning the plinth into concrete dust as it passed through it.

All was quiet for a moment. We started to breathe easily again, and I quickly let go of Rachel and the other cultist's hands. Rachel took a step forward, but just then the two halves of the Dark Stone on the floor, having survived the prior ordeal somehow, broke into smaller pieces again with a series of cracks.

Fortunately for her, Rachel took a step back to the wall, probably sensing something was about to happen. As soon as the sleeve of her robe brushed against my arm and her back was against the wall once more there was another crack.

It came from the rectangle this time, and a thin line had formed from the top of the rectangle to its bottom. The line gained several branches with another crack, and another, and another, until the entire rectangle looked like a spider web had been etched on it.

There was a brief moment of silence. I held my breath, knowing this was the calm before the storm. I was proven right when the rectangle burst outward, showering the room and its occupants in a spray of dust and concrete pieces. We covered our faces and our eyes with our hands, cringing backwards as the explosion continued until it finally stopped.

When the dust cleared, the concrete rectangle was completely gone. In its place was a rectangular space that was dark, and I couldn't tell how much space was in it. Rachel stepped away from the wall, shifting closer to the space gingerly.

"Is that...?" one of the cultists began to ask, his lowered voice loud in the quiet room before Rachel held up a finger to her lips. He stopped talking almost immediately. When she finally got within two feet of the space, she leaned over and peered in. Then she straightened up, looking around at the eager, curious faces around her and shaking her head.

Their shoulders fell in disappointment, but before she could say anything a pale hand shot out of the space and latched onto the ground around the space. Rachel shrieked and backed up until she was almost at the wall.

No one moved, and we watched as another hand, on the left side of the space this time, shot out of the darkness and grabbed the ground. The hands tensed, and there was a deep grunt before slowly, a head emerged.

My heart began to beat faster. *I know that voice.* I'd been speaking to the owner of the voice some minutes ago.

"Zalazar," I muttered under my breath. I was hoping the spell hadn't worked, but evidently it had. Rachel swiveled to face me, her eyes wide and crazed.

"You said his name. Is that him?" she demanded, leaning forward and into my face until I had to lean back to create some distance between us.

"I-I think so. It's his voice, anyway," I said.

Rachel's lips curled up into a wide grin, and she turned back to her fellow cultists.

"Our Lord has been awoken!" she cried, and they cheered. I'd never seen people so happy, except at a football match when their team won. These people were even happier... that their evil overlord was let loose on the world again?

They calmed down and turned back to the rectangle, which I'd realized was Zalazar's grave, waiting for something to happen. The head we'd seen shot upwards, the body following after, until we were all gazing up at a pale man hovering above the rectangle.

"He's a ghost?" I muttered to myself, wondering why there'd been so much talk about "reviving the Dark Lord" if he was just going to come back as a ghost. The cultists didn't seem to care though, as they erupted in what I could only describe as fanatical screams of joy at finally laying eyes on their beloved ancient cult leader. I could have sworn one of them even fainted, although I couldn't really say since the cultists kept moving forward to be closer to Zalazar, their large dark robes hiding anything behind them.

I looked over at Detective Grey. He was still being held down by two cultists, who I now knew were men, though I'd suspected it from their large builds. Their holds on his arms seemed loose, and they stared up at Zalazar in open-mouthed adoration. I wondered if we would be able to run away with all the cultists so distracted.

He met my gaze and shook his head sadly at me. I opened my mouth to say something and closed it without speaking. Even if I spoke, I doubted he would have heard me, and besides, what was I going to say—*Sorry for bringing back an evil Dark Lord to the world in exchange for my best friend's life, I didn't think it was actually going to work?..*

I tore my eyes away from his knowing gaze guiltily and looked back to Zalazar. Rachel had left her place near me and was now kneeling directly in front of Zalazar, looking up at him with teary eyes and a religious devotion that scared me. They'd been so dedicated to this person they didn't even know was real. *Is the Order so good at their job of indoctrination?* These people seemed like they would even throw themselves off mountaintops if Zalazar told them to.

Zalazar ignored the young woman kneeling in front of him, looking around the room instead. His eyes stopped on Detective Grey for a moment, a moment too long in my opinion, before they finally moved to the rest of the room. He took in the cultists who had all fallen to their knees, even the ones holding Detective Grey who had forced him to kneel too.

Then his gaze stopped on me, and my heart leapt into my throat. I was the only one standing, and one of the other two people not dressed in dark robes, meaning that I stuck out like a sore thumb. I was waiting with bated breath to see what he would say, but he simply huffed and returned his gaze to Rachel.

I slumped slightly, not sure if I should be thankful that his attention was no longer on me. He recognized me, that was for sure, but what did he intend to do to me?

There was nothing I could do but wait and see.

He threw his arms out on either side of him.

"My loyal ones," he boomed in a voice that shook the walls and hurt my ears. "I have returned!"

There was another round of cheers and screams, cut off abruptly when he raised his hand. Again I wondered at the power that he had over all of them.

"You have been faithful all this while, and you will be richly rewarded. I thank you for your service."

They nodded fervently, looking like they were ready to carry out any order he gave them. I shuddered.

19

ALIVE AGAIN

"Rachel, is it?" He looked down at her. She nodded, smiling from ear to ear. He beckoned her forward.

"You may stand. Come forward, so I may look at my loyal servant."

She did as he asked, stumbling to her feet and walking forward a few steps until she was almost at the edge of the grave.

"I have heard about your service to me," he said, glancing at me for a slight second, answering the question of how exactly he'd heard about her. I wondered with a shudder just how much he'd been able to glean from my mind. "I will give you anything you ask for. Just say the word."

Rachel's eyes gleamed with greed, and she nodded furiously.

"First, hand me the parts of that stone that were used to trap me," he ordered, gesturing at the pieces of the Dark Stone. Rachel quickly hurried to the spot where I'd dropped the Stone, picking up the pieces with such haste I wondered if she was afraid he was going to strike her down if she didn't hurry up. It would be on brand for him though, from the story Elena had told us of him.

Luckily for her, the pieces weren't too small, the stone having broken up into large chunks. She cradled the pieces in her palms and hurried back to where Zalazar floated, holding up her palms to him when she returned to her spot.

"Here, my Lord," she said breathily. He frowned down at the pieces, and I could almost see the chill creep up Rachel's spine as she leaned away from him slightly, probably afraid she'd angered him. *Luckily for her, something else is annoying him.*

"Hmph," was all he said as he waved his hands, levitating the pieces into the air and moving them around until they fit together in one perfect sphere again. The now restored Dark Stone hovered in the air in front of him for a moment, lacking its former luster, and the next moment it shot forward into his awaiting palm.

Part of me wondered how he could interact with the Stone when he was a ghost. The other part was morbidly curious as to what was going to happen next.

Zalazar eyed the stone in his hand for a moment with clear distaste, before his expression cleared and he looked back at Rachel.

"Now, my dear, what is it that you wish me to do for you, as thanks for your wonderful service? Don't be shy," he reassured her, seeing Rachel open her mouth only to bite her lip, seemingly hesitant. He sounded like a perfectly nice boss who only wanted the best for his subordinate, but a malicious part of me thought it was more likely that he wanted Rachel to get on with it and stop wasting his time, so he could get back to trying to enslave the world. *Or whatever his goal is.*

"Then," Rachel started, staring up at him with suspiciously bright eyes and a blush on her cheeks that got pinker the longer he looked at her, "Can I rule beside you?"

She got a raised eyebrow from Zalazar and scandalized gasps from the rest of the cultists still kneeling around us.

I was equally scandalized. *What was she thinking?*

"Oh, no, I don't mean to usurp your power or anything." She cut herself off as his eyebrow went higher and quickly corrected the course before she could put herself in trouble. "I just meant I'd like to be your queen," she said with a red face, making my eyebrows raise this time. "I would learn so much from you, and if you're going to rule the world you'll want someone to take care of the little things for you. I could do that."

She ended her pitch and looked up at him expectantly. The room was filled with murmurs, but she didn't even look over at her fellow cultists, eyes fixed firmly on the man.

To everyone's surprise, he began to laugh like it was the funniest thing he'd heard all day, or since he'd been defeated. *Maybe it was.*

When he finally stopped laughing his face grew serious and he eyed Rachel, who was clearly doing her best not to cower in fear. Then he smiled.

"But of course. I promised, didn't I? Everyone knows that Zalazar always keeps his word."

I wanted to point out that no one could verify that since everyone who'd actually known him was probably dead. It seemed the thought hadn't occurred to anyone else in the room, because they all cheered like they were the ones being elevated to a position of power. Rachel's smile returned to her face, and she looked up at Zalazar in anticipation, waiting to see what he would do.

We all waited. In the end, it was less dramatic than I'd expected. He asked if Rachel was ready. She nodded, and he waved his hand. That was all he did, before saying, "It is done."

There were some mutters in the room, which was quickly silenced when Zalazar glanced in the direction of the people who were murmuring. I stared at Rachel, wondering if she was disappointed. She was smiling though, even wider than she'd been when Zalazar had accepted to fulfill her name wish.

Does she know something we don't?

I looked at her closely. Nothing had changed, except that her hair seemed a little longer than it had been at the beginning. And were her cheekbones more pronounced? She looked like she'd gotten a facelift from an incredibly skilled plastic surgeon, but was that it? Evidently, Zalazar liked his women beautiful, but if I was Rachel I would be disappointed that that was all it amounted to.

Although looking at her again, I felt there was a weight to her presence that she hadn't had before. She looked more regal, standing straighter and now having the air of someone who knew they were superior in all aspects to everyone else. That was confirmed when she waved a hand and the dust and concrete pieces on the floor flew back into the rectangle to cover it again, becoming whole and solid again, with not one crack in sight.

There was a stunned silence before the cultists began to cheer again. Rachel dipped into a proud curtsey and then bowed low to Zalazar, who was floating in the air in front of her with a smug smile.

"Thank you, my Lord. I'll do my best to serve you even more," she said, still bowing her head.

He nodded and turned to me, waving Rachel away. She took the hint of dismissal and stepped back in line with her new subordinates, although they shifted to give her a wide berth so that there was a small circle of space around her.

"Now, Charlotte, do you still doubt me?" Zalazar asked, looking down at me. I shook my head.

"You said you would bring Diana back to life," I said in response, looking over at the other side of the concrete rectangle, where Diana's body lay. He turned in the air to look at the body too, then nodded and floated over to the body.

I followed after him, making sure to keep my distance from the cultists, some of whom were giving me nasty glares for whatever reason. I glanced at Detective Grey as I walked past him, but he only shook his head at me. I wondered if I was being led into a trap for a moment.

Would this end up as some sort of monkey's paw situation, where I would get what I wished for, only in a way that brought me sadness instead?

Well, whatever it was, it was too late to back out now. I'd come too far to go back, and I doubted Zalazar would look kindly on me for refusing the boon he'd so kindly granted me out of the goodness of his dark heart. Even more, I was looking forward to seeing Diana again. My teeth ached with anticipation, and I wiped my palms on my jeans. *When had they gotten so sweaty?* My heart started beating faster, and I couldn't think of anything but the thought of Diana alive again instead of hovering three feet in the air as a ghost.

Just like Rachel's makeover, Diana's return to life was equally anti-climactic. All he did was float down until his feet were on the ground again, and then he got to one knee, reached out, and touched Diana's forehead. He muttered a strange language under his breath, and took a step back, getting to his feet again.

"It's done," was all he said.

"Thank you," I said reflexively, before realizing nothing had actually happened. But as I looked at Diana's body, waiting for something to happen, a gust of wind blew through the room, causing our clothes to flap in the strong breeze and my hair to whip around my face. When I finally wrestled it back into control, the wind had stopped.

"What's going on?" a familiar voice said groggily, sounding like she'd just woken up from a deep sleep. I ran to my friend, who was sitting up, and tackled her into a hug, causing her to fall back onto the floor when she'd just sat up.

"Diana!"

I hugged her tightly, burying my face in her shoulder and inhaling the familiar scent of her apple-scented lotion. Tears left my eyes unbidden, and soon her shoulder was soaked with my tears.

She just patted my back, saying nothing. She didn't have to say a word. She was there throughout the maze, and she'd seen everything I'd gone through trying to bring her back. Some part of me realized that she would probably disapprove of my bringing back Zalazar just to get her back, but I couldn't bring myself to care. I would happily sit through any lectures she wanted to give me as long as she was still living. *This is all that matters.*

"As touching as this reunion is," Zalazar's uncaring voice drawled from above us, "I'm afraid we will have to cut it short. I and my followers have plans years in the making to carry out. Will you join us, Charlotte? I extend my previous offer to your friend too. She might not be as powerful as you are, but having more hands is never a bad thing."

I let go of Diana and helped her to her feet before turning back to face Zalazar. I was irritated at not having enough time to spend with my friend, but I reasoned that there would be more time later. At least I had her back now. I realized he hadn't made any mention of recruiting Detective Grey, and I wondered about it, even as I tucked the thought into a corner of my mind. I couldn't get distracted at that moment, and maybe he'd just forgotten about the other man.

"My answer is still no," I said.

Diana chimed in from behind me, "I don't think I'll be joining you either, sorry."

Zalazar shook his head in mock sadness. "That's a shame. We could have used your experience and expertise. Oh well," he shrugged, "if you are not with us, then you are not for us. Seize them."

I'd known this was coming, but I was still shocked at how fast the cultists burst into action. They swarmed forward to grab us, and Rachel, who'd been glaring at me ever since Zalazar asked me to join him once more, threw her hand out at us.

I felt a wave of malevolence rush towards us and I threw my hands up in front of us, moving purely on instinct. A translucent square shimmered into existence in front of us just as the wave reached us. It bounced off the square and onto the cultists who'd been rushing towards us, hitting them with such force they were thrown back against the wall on the other side of the room.

I ignored the sickening crack that echoed in the room when they hit the wall and turned to see what Detective Grey was up to. I was surprised to see him almost next to me the moment I looked. Glancing behind him, I saw the crumpled bodies of the two men who'd been his guards.

I looked at him. "Are you alright?"

He nodded at me. "I'm fine. Don't worry about me. Glad to see you, Diana." He turned to her as she blasted a wave of psychic energy at some cultists approaching us from behind. She turned her head to grin at him and returned to defending us.

He nudged my shoulder with his. I looked at him, trusting the shield in front of us to keep us safe for a moment.

"Can't whatever you want to say to me wait?"

He grinned and shook his head. "I just wanted to tell you that you're brilliant, and I'm sorry for doubting you. Also, we're going on date when we finally get out of here."

I turned back to the cultists rushing at us again, failing to hide the smile on my face. "I'm looking forward to it," I whispered before we plunged back into the fight.

For the first time since Diana died, things were looking up. Sure, we were surrounded by crazed fanatics on every side, but I'd never felt better.

Deep down, I know we are going to get through this.

20

———

LOST LOVE

Giddy from the promise Detective Grey had made to me, I threw myself into the fight with wild abandon. I didn't have any idea of what exactly I was doing or how I was doing it, but somehow I was doing it. I was throwing magic at anyone who tried to come near me... or Detective Grey.

For his own part he was doing pretty well, not that I expected any difference from someone who was trained in several different martial arts, throwing off any cultists who tried to jump on him and me.

Behind us Diana was doing pretty well for herself, using her psychic energy to protect herself from anyone who tried to attack her. I hadn't known she was able to use her psychic powers in that manner, but it made so much sense. She'd had some form of training and it was probably one of the things she'd learned.

The most surprising person, rather being, in the entire thing wasn't Rachel, who was coming at me with a fury I couldn't understand. She ignored every other person in my group, even Detective Grey, who she could take out permanently if she really wanted to, but she ignored every ounce of tactical reasoning she may have had to throw all her attacks at me instead. Was she playing the part of the jealous woman already? But what did she have to be jealous about?

I looked back at the true surprise in this battle. Where had Pearl come from? I had no idea if she'd been with us the entire time, or if she'd slipped in during all the chaos. Either way, she was darting from cultist to cultist, swiping at them with her unnaturally sharp claws and drawing blood most of the time. They had started to avoid her, opting to throw themselves at me, Diana or Detective Grey rather than have to face Pearl and her deadly claws.

I took a breath and paused. I hadn't used my magic before, but I was feeling the strain of continuously pulling on it and flinging it at whoever charged towards me. I knew I wasn't being efficient, and I was probably wasting more magic than I needed to, but it was the only thing I could do. I was starting to feel tired, and drained, and all I really wanted to do at that moment was lie down and rest. We couldn't rest until we'd eliminated the threat in front of us though, so I sighed and turned back to the fight.

I couldn't help but notice that Zalazar didn't seem to be too concerned with our fight, choosing to hover over the entire room and look down at us. His lips were curled up in amusement, although I couldn't say what was making him so amused.

"Think he's going to jump into the fight?" Detective Grey rasped beside my ear, panting beside me as he finally got a break for once.

I shrugged, keeping an eye on him even though he continued to do absolutely nothing but look down and watch us fight.

"I doubt it, but I don't like it. Let's just deal with these guys right now and then we can worry about him," I said. He nodded, patted me on the shoulder and jumped back into the fray.

Nearly ten minutes later, all three of us were exhausted, but the cultists looked much worse off. Even Rachel, although she was still on her feet, was panting, and she looked like she would faint at any moment.

"Can we get out of here now?" Diana whispered, leaning against me, her back to mine. Pearl had come over to curl up against my feet, licking her paws and looking like she hadn't even been winded. Apart from Zalazar, she was probably the only one in the room who still had some energy.

Zalazar floated over to us, slowly clapping.

"What a battle. I haven't seen anything like this since... hmm, probably the battle before those Oscuros scum locked me in that Stone for all that time."

We all took several steps back, which turned out to be of no use since he just floated over to us, ignoring our cautious glares.

"Just let us go, and we'll be out of your hair," Detective Grey bit out.

Zalazar turned to him, raising an eyebrow at him.

"Hmm? Tell me, why should I do that? You attacked my followers after I'd done the gracious favor of bringing your friend over there back to life. Even now you're still being ungrateful, demanding things you have no right to."

I was so annoyed at the way he'd twisted the events to fit his own narrative that I forgot I was supposed to be afraid and stepped forward, glaring up at him.

Detective Grey pulled at my sleeve, hissing at me to step back. I shrugged him off, not taking my eyes off Zalazar, who kept that infuriating smirk on his face as he looked down at me.

"It was your *follower* who killed my friend in the first place," I said, glaring at Rachel who stood just behind Zalazar. She narrowed her eyes at me, clearly unrepentant.

I furrowed my brow. "The same *follower* who then proceeded to trick me into coming down here and freeing you in exchange for my friend's life! We went through so much just to get here, and we did most of the work too. If anything, you should be thanking us for freeing you, because without my help you'd still be sealed by that stone."

I finished saying my piece and glared up at him. Rachel stepped forward, frowning at me, but Zalazar raised a hand and she stopped in her tracks.

"There's no need for more violence, my dear. We can let them go."

Rachel seemed even more surprised than I was at his words.

"My Lord? I don't mean to question you, but if we let them go they might go to the Oscuros–"

Zalazar threw his head back and laughed. The force of his amusement shook the walls again, and I finally remembered just who I was dealing with. I stepped back as casually as I could, and Diana quickly grabbed my hand, pulling me to stand beside her.

"Those scum? I can bet every ounce of my power that they don't have anyone as powerful as me currently. Back then? Of course. Right now? That's extremely doubtful. Let them come. I still have some revenge to serve them, after all."

Rachel nodded, smirking at me. "And what should we do with our guests, my Lord?"

He tilted his head, looking at us and thinking.

"We'll let them go," he said at last. Before Rachel could protest again, he added, "Not before we take what we need from them though."

I was fatigued all the way down to my bones, but I forced myself to stand straighter and get ready for any attacks that might come. Diana let go of my hand and went back to her position behind me. Detective Grey made up the third side of our triangle.

Zalazar scoffed at our efforts. "No need for that," he said, giving our actions a dismissive wave. "I'll get what I want without doing much."

I wondered what he meant even as I prepared myself to counter whatever he was going to pull, and just then Detective Grey grew stiff and fell to the floor.

I screamed his name and reached for him. Rather, I tried to, because just as I fell to my knees and reached for his face there was a firm, clawed grip on my arm, pulling me back to my feet and away from his jerking body.

I thrashed in the hold of my captor, but an audible sneer made me freeze and look around to see who it was. It was Rachel, of course. It seemed she was going to take any opportunity to hurt me, even though I was sure I'd never done anything to her besides being on a different side than she was.

"The Dark Lord is working," she hissed in my ear. "Don't interrupt him." What did his work have to do with giving Detective Grey seizures? I struggled in her grasp again, but she slapped me so hard my head snapped to the side and I felt like I was seeing stars.

Diana had been equally held down, although without the slaps. We watched as Detective Grey jerked uncontrollably for about a minute before his arms and legs finally stopped moving and he was sprawled out on the floor.

"Is he dead?" One of the cultists asked in a hushed voice. I didn't hear the answer, because I was looking for Zalazar.

It had occurred to me that I hadn't seen him in a while. I'd gotten used to his hovering over us mere mortals and just watching, so I hadn't thought much of it. But he'd said he would get what he wanted. Which brought me to the question: what did he want?

"Where's Zalazar?" I turned my head up to Rachel and asked. She scoffed at me.

"That's none of your business. He'll reveal himself in due time. Are you that desperate to see him?" she teased, though I got the sense it was more malicious than fun for her.

Detective Grey groaned and opened his eyes. I sagged in relief.

"You're alright," I sighed, not completely comfortable with Zalazar's absence, but at least I had my friend back again with me.

"Of course, I'm all right. Why wouldn't I be?" he asked. A chill shot up my spine.

Why was Zalazar's voice coming out of Detective Grey's mouth?

"Detective Grey?" Diana asked, exchanging a worried glance with me.

Detective Grey got to his feet haltingly, like a newborn fawn learning how to walk, but more gracefully. He shook out his limbs before turning to us with a wide grin that was out of place on that face.

"Detective Grey is not here. There is only me," he said with a smug smile.

My eyes widened. *No, no, please don't tell me that's–*

"Zalazar?" I asked, just to be sure. Deep down though, I knew it was the truth. Detective Grey wasn't the type of person to pull pranks, and even if he was, he wouldn't do it at such a serious moment.

Zalazar, wearing my friend's body, threw his arms wide open and grinned again.

"In the flesh," he said, giggling at the joke. "Surprised?"

"Get out of him!" I cried, wriggling out of Rachel's hold and rushing forward, magic at my fingertips. I held the intention to push the old sorcerer out of my friend's body and for a moment it worked.

When I touched his shirt and pushed him back I was quickly restrained again, this time by two men who made sure I couldn't get up and do something that would disrupt their plans again.

Zalazar shook his head and opened his mouth, but the voice that came out belonged to Detective Grey.

"Let me go!" he demanded, jerking his limbs all over the place. *Are they fighting for control of the body?* I was rooting for Detective Grey, although my hopes were soon dashed as the body stopped jerking.

"That one's a fighter," he said to me.

"Let him go!" was all I could say. He shook his head with fake sadness.

"I'm very sorry about all this. It's clear you cared a lot for him, but I can't just release him like you want. I have things to do, and a world to rule, and as much as I like my ethereal state I still need a physical body. He'll do quite nicely, as I can feel that he has some relation to me, and so our souls are similar enough for me to reside within his body."

He reached out, patted my cheek condescendingly, and said, "Don't worry, you'll get it back someday," before turning on his heel and walking out of the room and into the maze. The other cultists who weren't holding Diana and me down quickly rushed after him, and Rachel waited until he was out of sight before pushing me away.

"Don't bother coming after us," she said, a nasty grin on her face. "You'll just put yourself in unnecessary danger."

With that, she sauntered away. The man who'd been restraining Diana let go of her and raced after Rachel, leaving just the two of us alone in that room.

I didn't even flinch when the door leading into the maze shut behind them as they went. We could still leave through the door that led into my kitchen, although all I wanted to do was run after Detective Grey – now Zalazar — and shake him until Zalazar released his body.

"Charlotte." Diana placed her arm around my shoulder and tugged my torso towards her. I leaned against her as my tears began to flow.

I've been in love with that man for a long time, and I might never get to tell him?

"We'll get him back," Diana assured me. "Just like you did with me."

Time to gear up for the fight of my life...

If you loved this book, I'm sure you'll love my first series! Join me and Charlotte on her journey in Claws and Conundrums!

Get your copy <u>here</u>!

Claws, Conundrums, and a Curious Cat... Unleashing Cryptic Puzzles!

Little did I know that a mischievous tabby cat would become my ticket to freedom, using his uncanny ability to grant me visions and help me solve a perplexing murder where I'm the prime suspect!

As a discouraged New York City bookstore owner, I receive a mysterious letter claiming that Mr. Livingstone is leaving his sinister mansion in Picklesquare to me.

Greeted by the estate lawyer and neighborhood scapegoat when I arrive, I have to spend the night to clear things up with Mr. Livingstone.

Chaos erupts when I stumble upon the lifeless body of Anna, the estate's lawyer, the next morning. Faced with suspicion by the cute Detective Grey, the stoic cat leads me to the clues that will clear my name.

Danger looms as the cat and I form an undeniable bond and Detective Grey turns into an unlikely partner.

With each vision, we get closer to unmasking the truth and exposing the malevolent forces behind the pain hidden in the mansion walls.

Together, we delve into a web of intrigue, avoiding the watchful eyes of the real killer.

But meddling with the supernatural has consequences and we may not get out of this one unscathed...

Get your copy of Claws and Conundrums <u>here</u>!

Chapter 1: The Letter to No One

I've died and gone to heaven.

My mind is reeling from the notion that I just became the owner of a historic mansion overnight. This cannot be real.

I'm very certain that I'm not related to the owner of a mansion in a town I've never visited.

I mean, I don't think I've ever even met the guy! *This must be a joke!*

But two days after receiving a thick, official-looking envelope, I find myself driving to the small town where my sudden good fortune came from.

Picklesquare? Who names a town Picklesquare? Why don't people answer phones here?

"Ugh." I can smell the cabbie's breath from here. He's nice enough, but a shower would do him a world of good.

He suddenly slams on the brakes.

"What? Is something wrong?" I ask in alarm.

"Nothing ma'am. Just don't want to run over anyone."

"Huh?" It takes a second to register, but when I look out the car window, all I see are flashes of bright colors.

The town is buzzing with excitement, full of vibrant colors, loud noises, and yummy smells.

Impatiently, I silently wish the cab had a siren. I could check out the festival after getting to Mr. Livingstone's mansion. The town is as interesting as it is peculiar, but I need to get to him to get the answer to my seemingly random inheritance.

"Wha—?" Something catches my eye, and I turn my gaze to it.

A bunch of teenagers nearby are throwing rotten oranges at a black Ford in the opposite lane. They look mischievous and are laughing like it is the funniest thing ever to pelt a car with a rotten orange.

Boys. Who's driving that car? How enraged are they that they will now need to clean rotten fruit off their car?

I turn to look at the cabbie, David. He doesn't even seem fazed. He just chuckles and looks at me through the rearview mirror. He leans back. "People only throw rotten things at you if they hate you, you know."

I don't even like cleaning the dust or dew off my car.

I squint at the vehicle. "Who's in the car? The devil? Hitler incarnate?"

"I have no idea." The crowd finally thins out and he lurches the cab forward, jolting me back against my seat.

As the cab eases its way through the fading chaos of what I think is a Rotten Fruit Festival, my mind shifts to the task awaiting me at Mr. Livingstone's mansion. Two days ago, that unexpected letter arrived at my doorstep without an addressee.

Inside, I found a stack of documents bearing my name—titles to a grand estate just a few hours from my apartment. The top letter was odd and rubbed me the wrong way.

I hope this meets you in peace.

I am writing to you with a proposition of utmost significance. Enclosed within this envelope, you will find legal documents pertaining to the magnificent mansion of Mr. Livingstone. It may come as a surprise, but destiny has chosen you as the rightful heir to this grand estate.

You see, Mr. Livingstone has no immediate family. In his final moments of mental clarity, he entrusted me with the responsibility of locating the deserving owner of his beloved mansion. Through an extensive search and meticulous considerations, fate has guided me to you.

The moment I laid eyes on your name, I knew you were the one meant to inherit this glorious property. Your reputation as a person of integrity, wisdom, and compassion has reached far and wide, aligning perfectly with the values cherished by Mr. Livingstone throughout his life.

By signing the enclosed documents now, you will not only assume ownership of the mansion but also become the steward of its history and the legacy it holds.

Yours Faithfully,

Anna Butler

The Estate's Lawyer

As the cab jolts along the bumpy road, my mind wanders from "Where in the heck my reputation was the topic of conversation" to the serene view out of the cab window. I watch the scenery change from the chaos of the fruit festival to a serene and quiet atmosphere. David slows to a stop opposite the town center, and I peer out the window, my eyes widening at the sight before me.

A lofty double gate with an inscription mounted at the top and written in bold letters "LIVINGSTONE ESTATE" stares back at me. The grounds alone are magnificent. A spiraling wonder of bushes across the open gate makes me realize how poor I am living in the confines of my shabby two-bedroom flat in New York City. A straight cobblestone road lined with trees, their branches reaching out to form a natural canopy overhead, leads to the front view of the estate. Here, green ferns and plants line the area, adding to the jaw-dropping sight of the mansion further back on the estate.

This place is amazing, I think to myself as I gaze at the perfectly planted array. My eye catches a young man with heavily sun-kissed skin, tending to the garden on one side. He is tall with a muscled body that makes him look like a heavyweight champion. He waves at our cab and flashes me a friendly smile. *Does he wave at every single person who passes by the garden?*

The trees that line the road filter the sunlight, casting shadows on the ground as we move. There are also occasional benches and picnic tables inviting travelers to stop and take a break outside of the gate.

"Here we are." David makes an abrupt stop in front of the mansion.

I reach into my purse and pull out some money to pay. David chuckles again. "You don't have to worry about that. I'm glad you're in Picklesquare and I hope you enjoy your time here."

"Well, that's very nice of you." Grateful, I slide my last few dollars back into my wallet.

"But be very careful in this part of town. Mr. Livingstone's mansion is the last place anyone visits in Picklesquare." His face darkens and his eyes no longer glisten.

I frown at his statement. "What do you mean by that?"

But before he can answer, a car drives into the compound and stops directly beside the cab. A black Ford with bits of fruit on its windshield. *The car at the festival!*

Out steps a young woman with fiery red hair. Her face is scrunched up in a deep frown as though she has been forced to gulp something bitter. She mumbles some words to herself and backs away from the car as if it were a piece of trash.

"Excuse me," I call out to her, hoping to find out how to avoid such a fiasco myself. "Are you alright?"

The woman turns to face me, her eyes narrowing in annoyance. "I'm fine. Just another day in Picklesquare where kids love to throw rotten fruit at my car. Well, I guess I'm glad it didn't end up like the last time..."

The last time was worse than this?

The red-haired woman must have seen the look on my face, urging her to tell me what had happened the last time. Her face breaks into a tired smile. "I don't think you need to know about that now. I'm Anna Butler, by the way. You seem to be from out of town. What's your name?"

Anna!

Here is the estate's lawyer, the same person who sent the letter to me. *Surely, she knows what's going on!*

"Charlotte Miller," I reply, returning the smile and trying to hide my anxiety.

Her eyes grow to the size of saucers, recognizing my name. "Charlotte, huh? You're the one who inherited Mr. Livingstone's mansion, right?"

I feel the scrutiny of her gaze as she takes in my petite frame, from the dark brown curls that fall across my face to the tennies shoes that adorn my feet. "Yes, but I believe there's been a mistake. I'm not related to Mr. Livingstone or..."

Anna interrupts me. "Let's go in, shall we?"

Unable to interject, I follow her up the stairs as David sets my luggage just inside the door. He vanishes without saying goodbye.

As soon as I enter the huge doors to the mansion, I feel like I've time-traveled to a fancy 18th-century plantation! The entrance hall has a cool wooden staircase and fancy designs on the ceiling that look like they are from a fairy tale. Sunlight peeks in through pretty stained-glass windows, making the rugs on the floor bask in a rainbow explosion.

The drawing room is all vintage vibes, with cozy velvet couches, fancy tables, and chandeliers that scream "upscale party." And the dining room? Oh boy! It has a massive wooden table that has probably seen more food than a buffet line.

And Mr. Livingstone wants to give me all this?

It couldn't be worse than a nightmare. I wouldn't know how to preserve the rugs from the dust of my shoes nor would I know how to save the velvet couches from being stained with my breakfast or lunch.

"This has to be a mistake," I whisper, taking in the magnificence of the room again and again.

Anna raises an eyebrow, placing her jacket carefully on the back of the couch. An amused smile plays on her lips now. "You think it's a mistake? I've been waiting for you. Did you bring the signed documents?"

I frown, trying to make sense of her words. "But why would I inherit anything from someone I'm not related to? I don't even know what he looks like!"

"Ah, that's the million-dollar question though, isn't it? You signed the documents though, right? It's important that you signed them," Anna says with a forced smile.

"No, I haven't. I want to meet Mr. Livingstone because I do not intend to sign them. I still believe it is a mistake." I try not to shake.

Anna sighs, and I can see a frown returning to her face. *She is probably wishing the teenagers were still throwing rotten fruit at her. It would be better than facing an obstinate stranger who was rejecting a mansion!*

"Unfortunately, it's late now, and he doesn't receive visitors after sundown. You'll have to wait until morning. But I'll set you up in a room for the night."

"Very well. I suppose I understand. But I want to see Mr. Livingstone first thing tomorrow morning."

"That will not be a problem," Anna answers.

A sound soon echoes into the room where we are standing. I hear from the upper floor a "*tap tap*" that keeps on moving above us. I raise my head, "What's that?"

"Nothing," Anna quickly whispers, but I can tell from her voice that she is scared.

David's words ring in my head again. "*Mr. Livingstone's mansion is the last place anyone visits in Picklesquare.*"

The sound soon stops, again immersing us in the deep silence of the mansion's living room. I look at Anna but this time, her friendly smile is back on her face.

"Let me show you to your room." Anna walks out of the room.

We walk through a long passage that leads into the innermost part of the mansion. On each side of us, white stone walls adorned with intricate carvings line the passageway. The huge windows in the mansion go from the floor all the way up to the ceiling.

They must let in a lot of light during the day, offering a beautiful view of the outside scenery. It must make the rooms feel connected to nature.

"Here you go," Anna says as we get to a door in one of the hallways.

She opens it for me and steps aside while gesturing to me to go inside. Greeted by the warmth of a big room that could comfortably take in my entire one-bedroom flat, my eyes feel permanently stuck open now. The furniture is antique but well-maintained and retains its original beauty.

The walls are adorned with beautiful paintings and intricate tapestries, and the floors are made of polished wood that gleams in the light from the lamp. The room is glorious, a reminder of a bygone era, a time when elegance and refinement were prized above all else. The big bed in the room is large enough for five people to fit across it, but still, the room looks spacious.

As welcoming as the room feels, something seems a bit off. I shake off that feeling and continue touring the room with my eyes until Anna calls my name.

"Oh! Thanks," I reply as she opens the bathroom door on the left wall.

"The chef is running a warm bath for you. She wanted to welcome you to your new home. Also, tell her what you would like to eat for dinner."

I walk to the bed, running my hand over the comfy bedsheets. "Thank you." I sit down on the bed, barely knowing what to do with myself.

After a few minutes, a young lady in a white uniform and hair packed in a bun knocks quietly on the bathroom door.

"Your bath is ready, Miss Miller," she announces, a polite smile stretching across her face.

Just like the gardener, she has no problem beaming at me as though we've been friends since forever. *Maybe this place isn't bad after all.*

"It's Charlotte. Are you the chef?"

"Yes'm, Diana Milligan, the chef of the Livingstone estate."

Diana leads me into the bathroom where a tub filled with water is waiting for me. The water is steaming and the bubbles smell like roses. Diana leaves after I give a lofty dinner idea and I hurriedly get into the water. I take a breath and try to relax, letting the water wash away my stress from the journey. It is so quiet in the bathroom that I can even hear myself breathing.

The bubbles feel really nice against my skin, like a soft massage tending to the knots in my muscles. I sink into the water and sigh.

Slipping into a ratty band shirt and shorts from high school, I feel completely underdressed standing in front of the mirror at the sink. I don't think these could be real gold faucets, but the vanity could certainly be real marble.

I don't want to leave, but I guess I'd have to buy a new wardrobe if I wanted to stay...

I must have spent almost an eternity in the tub because Diana has set out my evening meal on the table already by the time I get back into the room.

How did she already make this? I really thought she was bluffing when she said she could make my favorite meal.

I lift the plate cover to reveal a tender, juicy steak with a thick mushroom sauce. Roasted garlic mashed potatoes and a blend of seasonal vegetables are on another plate, with a chocolate lava cake on another.

It is the meal of royals, and today, I'm definitely living like one!

One bite and my taste buds are immediately awakened by the explosion of flavors. The food is expertly seasoned, with just the right amount of spices and herbs. I can tell that the ingredients are fresh and high-quality and that the dish has been prepared with care and attention to detail.

Perfection! I could get used to this...

As I dig into the food, I question why the mansion still seems off, despite its friendly inhabitants. I can't wait to meet Mr. Livingstone and hand over the documents and be free from this whole mansion debacle.

Even if I were the rightful heir, how am I supposed to keep this place up?

As I eat, I think about every possible reason that made Mr. Livingstone choose me to inherit his mansion. Nothing comes to my head as a possible link to Picklesquare. Only my grandmother, who lived in this same town before her mysterious disappearance seventy years ago, could be a possibility. But my mom was taken to live with my aunt in Upstate New York shortly afterward, and we never came to visit this town after she had me.

Should I find Anna to say good night? She probably still hates me...

Thinking back to her car, I figure she might still be busy.

I'll just wait till morning to see her and Mr. Livingstone.

As I lay on my bed, my mind drifts to the life I have in New York City. I run a small bookstore, my sanctuary in the heart of a busy city. It is my haven filled with the amazing scent of old books and the soft rustle of pages turning. The cozy store is always adorned with stacks of novels, memoirs, and poetry collections, whispering tales of distant lands and captivating characters.

But it wasn't just the books that made the bookstore special. My cat, Clara, always lit up the place with her vibrant presence. Clara and I were like two peas in a pod, her furry paws always tagging along behind me.

This was until she died five months ago. Her death was a huge blow to me, and I haven't recovered from it. *I miss stroking Clara's fur and hearing her purr at the sight of me.*

But maybe things happen for a reason. Maybe fate has brought me to Mr. Livingstone's mansion for something I've yet to uncover.

Get your copy of Claws and Conundrums <u>here</u>!

Southern Style Sweet Fruit Tea

Ingredients

- 18 to 24 tea bags

- 1 1/2 quarts water

- 2 cups granulated sugar

- 48 ounces pineapple juice

- 12 ounces frozen orange juice concentrate

- 12 ounces frozen lemonade concentrate

- Lemon, for garnish, optional

- Mint leaves, for garnish, optional

Steps to Make It

1. Gather the ingredients.

2. Place 18 to 24 tea bags in bowl or pitcher. Pour 1 1/2 quarts of boiling water over tea bags.

3. Add 2 cups of sugar, stirring to dissolve. Let tea bags steep in sugar water for several hours or overnight.

4. Squeeze tea bags to wring out extra flavor before discarding.

5. Pour tea into a large bowl or pot. Add cans of pineapple juice, frozen orange juice, and lemonade.

6. Stir until the concentrate has thawed.

7. Pour equal amounts into 2 (1-gallon) jugs.

8. Add cold water to each jug to fill and refrigerate until thor-

oughly chilled, at least 2 hours. Shake well before serving. Garnish as desired.